W9-BIN-222

of Special Importance to our American Readers

The Case of the 24 MISSING TITLES ...

Over the years many of our American readers have been distressed that Harlequin Romances were published in Canada three months ahead of the United States release date.

We are pleased to announce that effective April 1972 Harlequin Romances will have simultaneous publication of new titles throughout North America.

To solve the problem of the 24 MISSING TITLES (No. 1553 to No. 1576) arrangements will be made with many Harlequin Romance retailers to have these missing titles available to you before the end of 1972.

Watch for your retailer's special display!

If, however, you have difficulty obtaining any of the missing titles, please write us.

Yours truly,

The Publisher
HARLEQUIN ROMANCES.

OTHER

Harlequin Romances

by VIOLET WINSPEAR

Many of these titles are available at your local bookseller, or through the Harlequin Reader Service.

For a free catalogue listing all available Harlequin Romances, send your name and address to:

HARLEQUIN READER SERVICE,
M.P.O. Box 707, Niagara Falls, N.Y. 14302
Canadian address: Stratford, Ontario, Canada.

or use order coupon at back of book.

BLACK DOUGLAS

by

VIOLET WINSPEAR

HARLEQUIN BOOKS   TORONTO
WINNIPEG

Original hard cover edition published in 1971
by Mills & Boon Limited, 17-19 Foley Street,
London   W1A 1DR, England

© Violet Winspear 1971

Harlequin edition published April, 1972

SBN 373-01580-1

The Harlequin trade mark, consisting of the word
HARLEQUIN and the portrayal of a Harlequin, is registered
in the United States Patent Office and in the Canada Trade
Marks Office.

Printed in Canada

CHAPTER ONE

SABRINA sailed to the island in a boat that looked as if it might be carried away by the wind halfway across. The boy understood her English and he sized her up, glanced at her suitcase, and indicated the small craft that rocked in the water off-shore. He carried her to his boat, splashing gaily through the shallows, and she sat among his fishing nets and watched the mottled green island, shaped like a curled-up anaconda, come slowly into view.

'Boss come soon, missie,' said the boy, pushing off and leaving her abandoned on the far side of the island, alone but for the insects shrilling in the overgrown banana bush and mango grass.

She had been informed by letter that someone would meet her, and she gazed hopefully around and tried not to feel too apprehensive about this post on a faraway island. She had come a long way and she didn't dare to face disappointment. She breathed the strange and spicy air, and gave a start as a brightly plumaged bird flew out of a tree that was a mass of creamy pompom flowers. The insidious tropical beauty struck at her senses, and she prayed that this job would be all right . . . offering interest and perhaps even a little happiness.

She felt the heat, and yet there was rain in the air, and she began to wonder if she was expected after all to find her way alone to the house of the Saint-Sarne family. There were no cabs in this remote area, but there was some cover from the rain offered by clustering umbrella pines across the road with an unpaved verge. The trees grew up a hillside which seemed to merge into vine-tangled jungle, holding Sabrina's gaze as she crossed the road. Suddenly a car shot from a fork in the road and bore down upon her like a streak of lightning. She was aware of turning startled towards it and it might well have struck her if the driver had not slammed on the brakes and skidded at an angle away from her. Angry eyes raked her, while she in her turn gave him a look of fury.

'Y-you could have run me down!' she cried out.

'You shouldn't stand gaping in the middle of the road,' he retorted. 'You pedestrians make me laugh, you jaywalk all over the place and car drivers take the blame when you get knocked down.'

'You drivers make me furious!' Sabrina's brown eyes seemed to burn when she was really aroused, and the good-looking driver of the sports car had an almost insolent look of liking and getting his own way. 'Some of you go crazy when you get behind the wheel of a car and turn every road into a hazard. You don't drive a vehicle, you aim a weapon!'

He sat there with an elbow on the wheel and slowly raised a blond eyebrow. Then he glanced across at the harbour and searched the front of it with his grey eyes. After a moment he returned his gaze to Sabrina, who now stood safely on the verge, a thin young figure in a suède coat, clutching the handle of her suitcase, and looking not unlike a hungry little cat turned out on a world with more kicks than kisses to give her.

'I'm here to meet someone,' said the young man. 'Don't tell me you're the new nurse?'

'My name is Sabrina Muir,' she replied stiffly. 'I am a nurse and I'm bound for a house called Snapgates.'

'And they do snap, Sabrina,' he drawled, his eyes narrowing to silvery slits as he studied her. 'Are you absolutely sure that you want me to take you there?'

'Of course.' She said it bravely because he looked at her so speculatively. 'I have been hired to attend the grandson of Mrs. Saint-Sarne. I have the letter in my pocket if you would like to see it?'

'I don't doubt who you are, as there appears to be no one else around with a suitcase and a dedicated air. All I am saying is that Black Douglas has had half a dozen nurses already, and some of them far tougher than you whom he sent packing within a few weeks. If you'll take my advice . . .'

'I wouldn't dream of taking the advice of anyone but the lady who has employed me. I don't know who you are, and I've certainly never heard of . . . Black Douglas.'

'Have you not?' The handsome male climbed from the car with a sleek grace and came in long strides to Sabrina's side. When he stood there he seemed very tall and she had to tilt her head to look at him. 'Black Douglas is the patient you have been hired to take care of . . . and when I say *take care* I mean it literally.'

Sabrina stared at him, and the thought stole into her mind that if he was a member of the Saint-Sarne family then it was a good job she wasn't pretty. He looked a devil with the women; outstandingly attractive and very much aware of the fact.

'The name you call my patient-to-be sounds a bit formidable for a child,' she said. 'Does devilry run in the family . . . you are a member of it, aren't you?'

A slow grin quirked his mouth and his eyes glimmered. 'Yes, I'm Ret Saint-Sarne . . . but, good lord,

7

you don't really believe that your patient is a child, do you?'

'I usually take care of children.' Her brow creased. 'I had no reason to think otherwise when I received the letter saying my nursing qualifications met with approval. I took it for granted that Douglas Saint-Sarne was a . . . a young boy.'

'He has never been a boy, in the sense that he played and reacted as a youngster. There has always been something of the black arts about him . . . a sinister air.' Ret Saint-Sarne lifted the suitcase she had lowered in sheer surprise. 'If you are really coming to Snapgates then we had better be on our way. Your patient can be as impatient as the devil.'

The rain was now drizzling down and Sabrina cast a rather doubtful look at the sky. She glanced across at the harbour and wondered if she wanted this job after all. She had always worked in London and with fairly young people, and it was obvious from what she had just been told that Mrs. Saint-Sarne had been deliberately reticent in her reply to Sabrina's application for the post. She had not mentioned that her grandson was a fully grown man!

Ret opened the door of the car and said not a word as he waited for her to make up her mind. Abruptly she slipped inside and heard him laugh softly as he went round to the other side and climbed in. His long leg brushed hers and she drew away before she could stop herself . . . then she blushed, for he was hardly the sort to flirt deliberately with a girl as plain as herself.

Her burn-coloured eyes, almost too big for her face, could not compensate for the quality she had of being as unnoticeable to men as a crocus in a field of daffodils. She had grown used to her own invisibility except when her skill as a nurse was needed, but it could still hurt when a man chose to tease her. The reason she liked to work with children was that early in her career while working at a nursing home she had overheard a male patient demand a prettier nurse than 'that mouse Muir with the hungry eyes'.

Sabrina sat tensely beside the driver of the vintage car, on her dignity as a skilled nurse and ready to answer smartly his teasing remarks.

'You haven't asked me how far we have to go,' he said.

'I was busy with my thoughts,' she replied. 'But I did rather gather from Mrs. Saint-Sarne's letter that Snapgates is an isolated house. It has a rather strange name, if I may say so?'

'Perhaps to suit a rather strange family,' he drawled. 'You will notice that traffic is infrequent along this road, which is one of the reasons why I can drive as if this were a racing track. The residents who used to farm tobacco and sugar cane have gradually sold up and moved off the island. Unlike my dour cousin, who is somewhat feudal ... he refuses persistently to let go his land, but I'd sell the lot if I owned it. He doesn't realize how wild it's running.'

'Is he too sick to go out much?' Sabrina asked, with a curious glance at the handsome profile of the man beside her.

'No, he isn't an invalid ... but I can't get over the fact that Aunt Laura led you to believe him a juvenile. I wonder why she did that? Maybe she thought you wouldn't come if you knew the truth.'

'The truth?' Sabrina's heart sank; had her premonition been right? Had she landed once again in a household of conflicting hopes and passions? 'I wish you'd be more explicit, Mr. Saint-Sarne, or does secretiveness run in your family?'

'It does,' he said frankly. 'It isn't my business to be explicit ... I was merely enlisted by Aunt Laura to meet you and act as chauffeur. She even told me not to make you nervous. She was being ironic, because Black Douglas will terrify the likes of you.'

'The likes of me, Mr. Saint-Sarne?' Sabrina gazed straight ahead of her and felt that old familiar ache of being thought unattractive. 'I am aware that I have no glamour with which to fight my battles, but because of it I may be tougher than you think.'

'Don't get me wrong, nurse. It won't matter to Black Douglas that you aren't a beauty. That's something he will fail to notice.'

'Then he sounds a most unusual type of man. In my experience most men judge the face before the character when it comes to women.'

'You sound a trifle sad, Nurse Muir. Did you choose to work in the tropics because some man has disillusioned you?' As Ret spoke a monkey darted in front of the car, skimming the wheels by the skin of its tail. 'If so, then you will interest my cousin, who has a dark and tragic side to his nature.'

'You don't much like him, do you?' As Sabrina spoke her gaze dwelt on Ret's hands, which gripped the steering wheel with something of anger. It sounded as if Douglas Saint-Sarne controlled the family fortunes, and Ret was quite obviously a young man who liked a good time. He would be envious of a cousin in good fortune and not the health to use it.

'Black Douglas and I are like sunlight and cloud, if I am not being too romantic for a nurse, who deals in realities? I am gaiety and he is storm. I am hard up and he is well off. Does that satisfy your curiosity, nurse?'

'You feel that fate owed it to you, the handsome one, to be in control of the purse-strings.' Sabrina had to smile. For it seemed to her that Ret was about as complicated as a spoiled boy. He was probably indulged by his great-aunt and dealt with more sternly by his cousin, whose appellation had a dark, stern ring about it. Douglas was the master of Snapgates. He was to be her patient ... and from the sound of it he was the complicated member of the family.

The sun through cloud was westering as they came in sight of Snapgates, a great rocky-looking house, the sunset burning like ancient fire behind its gables and patrician columns and carved roofs.

The car was so powered that it took the upwinding road with effortless speed, advancing every second towards that lonely-looking house that overlooked canefields and wild land owned by Black Douglas, whose name clung tenaciously to the mind of the young nurse who had not yet made his acquaintance.

They had almost reached the house when Ret suddenly braked by the roadside and turned to face Sabrina. She felt the slumbrous energy in his gaze, while all around them the gathering dusk and the homeward flying birds gave to the landscape a sombre air.

'There it is,' said Ret. 'It could be made attractive, but my cousin has no eye for beauty, as I told you earlier on. It's all wildness and birds flying in from the reefs. The windows at the back of the house overlook the sea and at night you can hear the ebb and flow of the tides, the splash of water over the reefs, echoing in the groynes that connect with the cellars, used long ago to hide contraband and rebels from the uprisings.

There has long been a dash of venturesome blood in the family veins.'

This statement did not surprise her, and as she gazed at the house the sun died down to a soundless glow, strange and sombrely lovely seen through the rain.

'Why is your cousin known as Black Douglas?' Her eyes dwelt intently upon Ret's face as she asked the inevitable question. He gazed back at her with a slight frown and tapped his fingers upon the steering wheel. His white suit was impeccable upon his lean body; he wore his fair hair rather long and his sideburns glinted against his tanned skin. He was incredibly good-looking, yet Sabrina felt no stirring of her pulses. It was as if she could no longer be stirred by any man; as if their indifference had left her quietly intact in her shell. It amazed and even pleased her that she could look at Ret Saint-Sarne with such cool eyes, curious only about the dark master of Snapgates.

'There are some people who can't be explained to a stranger,' he said. 'You must meet him yourself and decide how he strikes you. The name has been his for as long as I can remember ... these days it's more appropriate than ever.'

And having mystified Sabrina still further he started the car and drove towards the house. The tall gates of scrolled iron were closed and Ret pressed on the motor horn until a man came running from the gatehouse, clad in black trousers and a white cotton jacket, the sleepy-looking keeper of the gate and the grounds. He stared curiously at Sabrina as he unclosed the gate and the car swept past him. She gave a jump at the clang of iron behind them and saw ahead of them a shadowy drive snaking among tall trees. They seemed to travel along this corridor of shadow for about ten minutes, then suddenly they turned into the courtyard of the house. As the car came to a halt in front of a row of stone pillars a peacock cried in the dusk, either as a welcome or a warning. Sabrina was out of the car before Ret and almost without thinking she ran up the steps and stood in awe against one of the gigantic columns. They reared upwards, holding aloft a veranda, which was smothered in bougainvillea.

It was a strangely built house, a mixture of the classic with the rough, as if each successive master had added something of his own personality.

Ret strolled up the steps carrying her suitcase, look-ing quite like the handsome knight who would safeguard her from the dragon ... if she had been pretty and clinging and helpless as her thin body sug-gested.

There were wrought-iron lanterns alight along the colonnade and by their light Ret gazed into Sabrina's large eyes. 'I can see that the house intrigues you,' he said. 'Black Douglas's hideaway from the world in which at one time he was very much involved.'

'You make him sound an ogre,' she accused. 'Can't you have a little pity for him when you own such splen-did health yourself?'

'Pity Black Douglas?' Ret gave a mocking laugh. 'You'd better not do so, nurse, or you'll be sent packing before you've been here a day. In this house there is a cardinal rule ... we all pretend that he's just like other men.'

'Why, isn't he?' she gasped, picturing a sort of mon-ster.

'No.' Ret spoke seriously. 'I've never thought him quite like other men.' And with these mystifying words Ret led her into the house through french doors, and

13

there opened before her a vast room with a marble floor, alcoves in which stood pieces of statuary, and at its centre a staircase leading in graceful swoops to a long gallery.

'I've had a long train journey,' said Sabrina, 'I'd rather like to freshen up before I meet Mr. Saint-Sarne.'

Ret flicked his eyes over her face and hair, but he didn't say what he was obviously thinking. Her meeting with Black Douglas had to take place, and with or without make-up she would not impress him with her appearance.

Ret took hold of a bell-pull and within a minute a manservant appeared in the hall. 'Charles, which rooms have been assigned to Nurse Muir? The usual ones?'

'Yes, sir. Shall I take up the young lady's suitcase and show her the way?'

Ret stood hesitant, abstracted, as if he were listening to something other than the question addressed to him. He was about to speak when Sabrina caught the sound as well ... that of a walking-stick on the marble floor at the shadowy end of the hall, beyond the staircase with its balustrade of lacy iron.

Ret was facing that end of the hall, while Sabrina was facing Ret. She could see his face clearly and the expression upon it, a mingling of fascination and hate!

Even as she stared at Ret's face she heard footsteps approaching behind her, deliberate, almost lazy, as a master would walk in his own house. Sabrina wanted to turn with a look of poise to greet him. She wanted this first meeting with Douglas Saint-Sarne to go with ease, but the things his cousin had intimated were not easily put out of mind and she could feel herself standing stiffly like a waxen figure, while inexorably those footsteps came nearer. . . .

Then so suddenly that he scared her Ret reached out and pulled her to his side. 'Watch out! He'll hit you with that stick!'

Eyes wide and startled, she faced the man who was to be her patient . . . he was dark, almost swarthy, and taller than Ret, with shoulders in proportion to his height. He wore a smoking-jacket with a spill of ash, and his black hair was untidy above his dense black brows and a pair of grey eyes with a strange radiation to them.

Black Douglas . . . his left hand gripping tensely the handle of the white walking-stick!

Realization struck at Sabrina like a blow. The eyes that seemed to look right through her, cutting her to the core with their cold brilliance, were the sightless eyes of a blind man. It was unbelievable, and yet it was a cruel fact. Douglas Saint-Sarne sensed her standing there but he could not see her. The nostrils of his rather imperious nose twitched slightly, as if he breathed the delicate perfume she was wearing. His powerful, almost noble head reared back slightly, like a stallion in blinkers.

'Ret?' the voice was deep, stern, cultured. 'You have arrived back from the harbour with my latest Nightingale?'

'Yes, the nurse is with me.'

'Does she speak?' queried the man, who could not have been very much older than Ret yet who looked as if suffering had matured him. Deep lines grooved his face. He was sardonic, harsh with the world he could no longer see. Sabrina knew from the look of his eyes that he had not always been blind. It had come suddenly, and because there was no mark of a scar it had come from within that proud head ... yes, it was that kind of a head, with a clever brain in it, and pain which had cleaved a pit between the strongly marked brows.

'It would be a trifle confusing for a blind man to be led about by a nurse without a voice,' he added in his sardonic drawl.

'Of course I can speak.' Sabrina was shaken but determined to stand up to him. 'How do you do, Mr. Saint-Sarne?'

'Ah, so I have a young one this time! And you can *see*, nurse, I walk in darkness and tread the path of the damned and the doomed, but my ears are sharp. How do you do?' He held out his right hand, which looked strong enough to crush her fingers! She couldn't help hesitating a moment before placing her hand within his. He held it instead of shaking it and ran his thumb over the supple young skin. He seemed to be brailling the fine bones and slender shape, as if her hand could give him some idea of her person.

'I judge you are dedicated to your mercy mission?' he said. 'Ah, your hand tensed angrily then. You have, I believe, a bit of a temper. Muir? It's a Gaelic word for sea, isn't it?'

'I believe so, sir.' She spoke stiffly, for he ruthlessly suppressed the pity she might have felt for him. Just to look at him was to sense the power of his personality. Black Douglas had the name and the looks of a necromancer, with elements of the tragic lurking about his strongly defined mouth. It was also a rather sarcastic mouth and Sabrina was braced for his remarks as if she were a witness for her own defence.

'Are you a Gael?' he asked, releasing her hand and leaving his touch upon it. 'I don't mean one of those

16

elements which blow the tiles off the roof.'

Sabrina's hand tingled . . . his was a face which asked to be slapped.

'It might amuse you to hear that I was a foundling,' she said, with a touch of dignity. 'The name Muir was sewn into my clothes, and the director of the home added Sabrina to it. I . . . I don't know why.'

'Sabrina the ill-fated nymph.' As he spoke Black Douglas arched one of the brows that shaded the cobalt-grey eyes. He was mocking her, and he was also warning her that fate had not been kind in bringing her to Snapgates.

'Ret,' he half-turned to face his cousin, 'you will show Nurse Muir to my study. I am about to go and call Brutus. He took a run a while ago and I don't want him chasing monkeys and developing a blood-lust.'

'I don't know why you keep the brute,' Ret retorted.

'Because he is my seeing-eye, cousin. My only real companion, when all is said and done. He tolerates my temper and remains loyal. We match each other, Brutus and his Caesar.' A faint smile played over the saturnine features. 'And shall I call you Cassius, cousin?'

Sabrina glanced at Ret and it amazed her to see a blush darkening the fair skin. His look was almost guilty, as if he did plot the overthrow of Douglas, master of this great house on a rocky bluff above the tropical ocean.

'We go this way,' he said to her, and as they walked to the far end of the hall Sabrina realized that the manservant had gone with her suitcase to the upper regions, and very soon she would be left alone to face the most challenging patient of her career.

Ret swept open a pair of carved doors and ushered her into the study. 'I'll leave you here as he wished. Don't look too nervous. He may not be able to see you, but he has a devilish quick ear for a quaver in the voice. Relax and take a chair. Why be afraid of a man who couldn't catch you even if he felt like chasing you?'

'Don't be cruel,' she rejoined. 'It can't be any joke for a man of such vitality to be sightless. If he's impatient with people who can really condemn him?'

'Nurse, he was never all that gracious! Now I'll leave you to await his dark lordship. See you later.' He bowed out mockingly and closed the doors deliberately behind him.

Sabrina gave a slight shiver and walked away from the cool swirling of a large ceiling fan. The room was high and handsome, and she felt quite small as she stood there and wondered at her own audacity in taking a post so many miles from all she had ever known. It seemed unbelievable that here she was, on an island on the Coloured Lake.

CHAPTER TWO

WHILE Sabrina awaited her patient she took from her pocket the letter which his grandmother had written to her. As she read it by the light of the lamp which she switched on she wondered why it mentioned not a word about his blindness.

'There are times,' ran the letter, 'when he is quite active and shows no sign of pain, but there are other times when he needs his pain-killer and I cannot bear to give him the injections. Your qualification has been approved by our family physician, who will see you when you have settled in at Snapgates to give you the history of the poor boy's illness. Caring for him will not be too tiring for you. He can dress himself and manages to eat his meals without help. . . .'

It was Mrs. Saint-Sarne's use of the word 'boy' and her reference to him being able to dress and eat without assistance which had led Sabrina to think him a child.

He was far from childhood . . . and perhaps not so black by nature, if his grandmother cared for him so much. Of course, Sabrina had to admit, love was often blind, but it could be that Black Douglas accepted from his grandmother the compassion he rejected from others.

Sabrina gazed at the carved figure of an ancient god on a low table; its face was incredibly alive, but its eyes stared blankly into space. As she wondered if she would be able to cope with a blind and embittered man, she caught the sound of his stick on the marble floor outside the room. She tensed as he groped for the handles and pushed open the doors. He stood tall and dark in the aperture, and the unnerving blind grey eyes were full upon her as he closed the doors behind him and came unerringly towards her.

Now that Sabrina was entirely alone with Black Douglas she realized forcibly that before the onset of his blindess he would not have been a man to shut himself away from the world. As curiosity stabbed at her, and she could look directly at him without being observed, she wondered why a man with such a large house and the money to upkeep it had never married. Was he a woman-hater? Or had he loved someone and been rejected when he became blind?

'You don't speak,' he said, in that deep almost merciless voice. 'What are you doing, summing me up and wondering how you'll tolerate my affliction? I am not a patient man, nurse. I won't be led around by the hand, or pitied. I have all my faculties barring the one, and you will only be needed when I develop one of my foul headaches. Well,' his nostrils flared, reminding her again of a stallion on a rein he hated, 'do you think you have the nerve to cope with such as me?'

'I've coped often enough with stubborn children, so why should I tremble at the thought of managing you, Mr. Saint-Sarne?'

'Brave words, nurse! I wonder if you can live up to them? I'm hardly a child, as you can see.'

'Far from it,' she agreed. 'I am merely pointing out that if I have had patience with mettlesome children, there is no reason why I should get into a flap when it comes to looking after you. Are you such a tyrant?'

He stared towards the direction of her voice, and once again it came as a shock that those penetrating eyes could not see her. 'There is a dash of daring in the Gaels, and something in your voice, some suggestion of a lilt, tells me that you were a fey foundling, Nurse Muir. My ears are sharp though my eyes are blank, which can be disconcerting for people who think they are safe from my observation.'

'I'm sure, sir, that you miss very little of what goes on at Snapgates.'

'You are pert, miss. One of those young madams who go in for nursing in the hope of landing a big fish. Let us get something straight from the start ... I can't be charmed by a lilt in a voice.'

'I never supposed you could sir. But as it happens I became a nurse because I happen to like the work, not as a short step to matrimony.'

'You are a career woman, eh?'

'I like to think so, Mr. Saint-Sarne.'

'And do you happen to think you'll like working here? Look around you. In my mind's eye I can still picture each detail of this room, and everything is kept exactly in its place so I shan't fall on my face. Do you find it an attractive room?'

She looked at the finely panelled walls, the marble fireplace, the deep red damask at the long windows. She noticed how the furniture was arranged close to the walls to provide ample room for a blind man to move about without stumbling. Lamps with silk shades stood on the sofa tables, but he would have no use for them. Books crowded a marquetry cabinet, but they were no longer read by him. Only a large chair with a dented cushion gave evidence that the room was ever occupied ... and of course the fan was cooling the tropical air.

'Between the windows hangs a portrait, nurse. Take

a look at it and you will see me as I used to be.'

Sabrina glanced upwards at the framed portrait of a powerful figure in riding clothes seated upon a horse whose mane was as wild and black as the man's hair. Horse and rider blended into a background of wild land and cloud, and there was in the grey eyes an alive and leaping look. The painting was so vivid that the horse seemed about to leap out of the frame at the flick of the master's whip.

'That is what you'll have to contend with, nurse, a man who was extremely active and who is now restricted to a walking pace. It limits my patience; it makes me roar at times like a caged animal. What do you say to that?'

'That you seem rather like a black-maned lion.' She allowed a smile to slip into her voice. 'They always seem the most dangerous to me.'

'Dangerous, eh? Does that mean you are already afraid of me?'

'I believe you like people to be afraid of you . . . their fear makes it possible for you to stay aloof from them.'

'How perceptive of you to realize that.' He moved his stick so that it touched her shoe and he could therefore judge how near she was to his dark and towering figure. 'Why don't you sit down? There is a chair at your side almost.'

It was the velvet winged chair in which she would feel lost and at a disadvantage in parrying his edged remarks. She took instead a heavy, stiff-backed chair. 'Won't you sit down yourself, Mr. Saint-Sarne?'

'Why, because I'm blind and ailing?'

'No, because you make my neck ache to look up at you.'

He laughed dryly and found the chair with his hand. His dark fingers clenched against the velvet, and then he sat down and the effect of his black-clad shoulders and his dark head against the red was startling. Sabrina realized she was staring and she at once looked away as if he could see her.

'Have you nursed in a Caribbean house before?' he asked, and this made her look at him again and she saw that his hand was searching by his side for the table that stood there, and the cedarwood box that stood upon it. Those strong, dark fingers found the lid and pushed it back and he took from the box a crisp-leaved cigar. She could hear the faint rustling of the rolled leaves in his fingers. 'I hope you don't mind the aroma of a cigar, Nurse Muir?'

'No – not at all.' A man had never said such a thing to her before and the remark confused her. It implied a strange intimacy and she was suddenly aware of the close relationship a nurse developed with her patient, and this would happen with Black Douglas ... if she stayed here. She continued to watch him in a fascinated way as he lit the cigar from a cylinder lighter that pressed right in against the tip and set it glowing. Smoke drifted from his nostrils and his features seemed to relax.

He was as independent as he could be ... he wouldn't ask for a light, and therefore it must try his patience that upon occasion he had need of a nurse to give him those pain-killing injections, and to look after him when the pain laid him low.

'About working here on the Coloured Lake?' he said. 'Is it an innovation for you? I seem to get that impression.'

'It is,' she said. 'I've always worked in London. I'm a

23

city sparrow.'

'I used to be in business in the city of London myself,' he drawled, 'but I was referred to as a hawk with a sharp eye for a deal.' He drew hard on his cigar and his brows made a black bar above his sightless eyes. He seemed to smoulder inwardly at the cruel trick of fate which had taken from him his clear, shrewd sight.

Blinded hawks cannot fly,' Sabrina thought, and she felt a stirring of that compassion he hated so much.

'The drive from the harbour must have shown you that we are a good way from the township and places of entertainment. Will you be bothered by this, that Snapgates is somewhat isolated and overlooks the sea?'

'It will make a change for me,' she replied. 'I shall be able to explore and go swimming in my spare time.'

'The waters surrounding this island are sometimes treacherous and it would be as well if you didn't try to cope with an undertow as well as a blind patient. If you got into difficulties I couldn't play the hero, and Ret is not apt to risk his neck for the sake of my nurse.'

Sabrina couldn't suppress a wry smile. Black Douglas had few illusions about people and he didn't intend at this stage in his life to collect any. He couldn't see Sabrina, so he assumed her to be a pretty piece in a nursing cap intent on flirting with his handsome cousin. Words would not convince him that she was a creature of duty; he was the sort of man who believed only in deeds. Sabrina glanced around the room in which he now lived with memories of his own deeds, and when he spoke again she gave a jump.

'We will discuss your duties.' He said it sternly, resentfully, as if the fact of her whipped at his male independence. 'Did my grandmother brief you on what ails me?'

'She told me very little in her letter. I did rather get the impression that you were . . . younger.'

'You hesitated over that word. Do I strike you as ancient?'

'No, but you are older than I believed you to be. Until now I have always looked after juvenile patients.'

'So you came to Snapgates believing your patient to be a mere boy? It must have come as quite a shock to be confronted by a man in his thirties, and blind to boot!'

'It was a bit of a shock,' she admitted. 'But I'm rallying.'

'Excellent. But having just learned that you are a children's nurse I should like to be told your age . . . if I am not being too ungallant?'

'You are rather ungallant, but I suppose we are expected to excuse you because of your affliction?'

'Your age, miss?'

'I'm twenty-three, sir.'

'How very youthful. Are you qualified?'

'Fully. I started nursing at the age of seventeen . . . at least I wore my fingers to the bone scrubbing out things in the sluice room.'

'It hardly sounds romantic. But it really was remiss of Nan not to tell you that my only childish trait is that I sometimes spill things.' Ash dropped from his cigar as he spoke and spilled on the black brocade of his smoking-jacket. 'However, I shan't need to be sung to sleep, or to have my bruises kissed. Think you can cope? If not be frank and say so.'

'I believe I can cope, if you will try and be a little patient with me at first.'

'I am the patient, nurse.' He spoke dryly. 'My temper has always been a bit on the volcanic side, just to warn you in advance, and I have a tendency to demand coffee at ungodly hours of the night. I like also to take an occasional drive, but Ret and I don't click. I hope you can drive?'

'Yes, I have a driving licence.'

'Good. I take it you can also drive in the needle without making a man yell blue murder? One nurse I had was about as gentle as a motor mechanic.'

'Are you squeamish then, sir?' A tiny smile came and went on Sabrina's lips. It was an odd fact that men who could bear great pain were those most liable to kick against the small pricks, and Douglas Saint-Sarne had the look of such a man. He might surmount a high peak, but he would grumble like the devil at the mere stone in his path that he could not see to kick away.

'And you, nurse? Why do you take a job out in the blue and ask very few questions about it? What drove you here, like a piece of leaf-coral on the tide? A broken romance?'

'No.' She spoke bravely, though the colour had left her face. This man sensed the things which he couldn't see, and he knew her to be on the run from something intolerable. 'I felt I needed a change and when I saw your grandmother's advertisement in the *Nursing Mirror* I took the plunge and answered it. To work on a Caribbean island took my fancy, as well as the name of your house. And when I saw the house for the first time I was not disappointed. It's quite beautiful in a mixed sort of way.'

'Beauty should be mixed, not a thing of formal boredom. Like music it should have changing notes and themes. Before I became blind I took music for granted, now it has become one of my few ways to find solace. Am I boring you?' He paused and seemed to look right at her in that confusing way of his ... she would not have believed that sightless eyes could be so direct.

'Not in the least, sir. I'm very interested.'

'Are you, nurse? I can't see your face and voices can be deceptively sweet, but I do know that when a man becomes blind there are women who find him tedious. A man minus his sight can no longer admire a new gown or hair-style; he can no longer flatter because it would sound false. Pretty speeches in the moonlight take on absurdity because his kind of night has no moon. He rages against pity because it is all he can expect ... especially if the woman happens to be lovely.

'Nurse,' his voice went soft and almost dangerous, 'are you very attractive?'

If he had suddenly reached out and slapped her Sabrina couldn't have been more stunned. Oh, how easy it would have been to lie to him, to say that she bowled over every man who looked at her, but with calm truth she replied: 'No, sir. I'm quite ordinary.'

'You're remarkably modest for a female.' His dry smile deepened the lines beside his mouth and his eyes. 'Then let me be honest with you, so that when my blindness puts me into a black fury you will understand and just leave me alone. I can't tolerate fuss, and being dependent on people. Not being able to see if my tie's straight, or if I'm wearing a pyjama jacket to go into town.'

Sabrina laughed before she realized that she ought

27

to cry ... yet he would have stormed at tears, and when he heard her laugh a sardonic smile changed the ironic set of his lips.

'It's strange that we should laugh about it, eh? Better than weeping, which only gives a girl pink eyelids. D'you like dogs, because I can hear Brutus snuffing at the closed door. He's black as the devil, like me, but if you're going to stay here then you'd better get used to him. Go and open one of the doors and I'll call him to me ... he'll bound in like fury itself, but I don't think he'll bite your head off. You're not a redhead, are you? One of my nurses was and he didn't like her very much.'

'No, my hair isn't red.' Sabrina rose to her feet and knew that Black Douglas was testing her nerve by telling her to admit his seeing-eye dog. They could be gentle, but Ret had called this one a brute. She braced herself and walked to the door. She opened the left side, almost blindly, and jumped hastily from the path of the Shepherd, large, black and furry, who bounded in and made for that wing-chair in a fog of cigar smoke.

A hand reached out and patted the dog, who whined his affection but did not jump at the man. He had been trained to respect the needs and restraints and instinctive fears of a blind master, but after greeting his master Brutus turned to eye Sabrina with bristling suspicion.

'You can cut that out,' Black Douglas ordered. 'The new nurse tells me she isn't a redhead, so she must be a blonde or a brunette. Is she a blonde, old lad?'

Determined to show she wasn't afraid of these two, Sabrina moved from the door towards the chair she had left. The dog growled and at once the lean hand sought its collar and tightened on it. 'Be still, Brutus. Are you jealous because I have a new nurse? And you, nurse, don't be afraid. Speak to him. Say his name.'

'Hullo, Brutus,' she said, forcing herself to speak calmly in the face of the guardian Shepherd with fierce eyes fixed upon her. 'You're a handsome boy, aren't you? Come, let's make friends.' She held out a hand and all the time Black Douglas watched as if he could see, and perhaps he could in his mind's eye. Perhaps he pictured a blonde and beguiling creature who liked all male creatures to like her. Sabrina only knew that if she was to make a success of this job she must win over the seeing-eye dog. He was, and he seemed to know it, the most important member of this household in so far as Douglas Saint-Sarne was concerned. A blind man living in a rambling house above the sea could not rely entirely on a stick. The dog was here to guide him up and down the cliff paths . . . a fall from the cliffs might easily kill him.

Brutus eyed the hand she held out to him, and no one would ever know how fast her heart beat when the dog cocked his ears and put forward his nose until its damp coldness was touching her skin. He sniffed her fingers and she expected any second to have them snapped at by the canine teeth.

Then to her utter relief Brutus licked her hand and gave her such a quizzical look that she laughed shakily. 'I hope that's a kiss of welcome,' she said, 'and not a taster before you take a bite.'

'I think you'll find, nurse,' drawled Black Douglas, 'that Brutus has taken to that little bit of Blarney in your voice. I bought him from a kennel over in Ireland where dogs for the blind are trained by a woman friend of mine. She lives in an old castle in Killarney and

Brutus is attuned to catch the lilt in the voice. Be glad you have it.'

'I certainly am if I'm to share a patient with a black Shepherd.'

'Do you think we suit each other, the dog and I?'

'Without a doubt, sir.'

He laughed in that ironic way of his and fondled the dog's handsome head. 'You must be in need of some coffee after your trip from the mainland. Did you fly from London?'

'Yes. A boy brought me to the island in his fishing boat. It seemed so flimsy that I thought it would capsize and I'd be thrown into the water. I can understand why the water around the island is called the Coloured Lake. It's all shades of blue and green.'

'Yes, like a gem,' he drawled. 'But it wouldn't do to be capsized into it. There are sharks lurking underwater. They swim around the reefs, where shoals of small fish haunt the coral, and in the days when I could sail a sloop without jamming it on the rocks I often saw barracuda out there in those coloured waters. Beauty can be deceptive. It can hide things.'

Having said this he indicated that she pull the bell that hung by the wall. 'We will have coffee together, nurse. You're going to have to get used to my company and the sooner you start the better. You said your first name was Sabrina, didn't you? The ill-fated nymph!'

'It was you who said that, sir.'

'Yes, and it may be truer than you think – and for heaven's sake stop calling me *sir*. You make me feel like a teacher with a cane! You had better call me Douglas ... though doubtless the appellation will be added when I am not within earshot.'

'I shouldn't dream . . .'

'Don't go on with that statement, Sabrina. Of course you dream! All girls do, about love and other such nonsense.'

Before she could reply that love was something she had put out of her mind, Charles tapped and entered the room, and was requested to bring coffee and cakes right away.

'Those coconut things, Charles, with the marshmallow.'

'Of course, sir.' Sabrina saw a slight smile flicker across the man's dignified face. 'And perhaps some ginger cake?'

'By all means some ginger cake.' Black Douglas seemed in his uncanny way to find Sabrina in his blindness and to fix his clear grey eyes upon her. 'Though I have a suspicion, Charles, that my new nurse has already some ginger in her. Tell me, is her hair red?'

Charles glanced at Sabrina with a haughty sort of amusement. 'Nurse Muir is on the fair side, Mr. Douglas.'

He should, in Sabrina's opinion, have said nondescript, but to say she was fair was to paint a picture which might appeal to the dark Douglas. Sabrina knew in advance how painfully it would hurt if Ret were to tell him the blunt truth. 'She's plain, old man. The sort of girl you don't even notice, unless you need an aspirin.'

CHAPTER THREE

SNAPGATES, so Sabrina found in the days that followed her arrival there, had a tropical graciousness about it that belonged in lots of ways to the past. When King Cane ruled these islands and the sugar knives swung in the sun and smoke and flame belched from the chimneys of the rum and sugar mills. Now they were quiet, those belonging to the 'great house' as the staff called the white-stoned, irregular dwelling with its curious beauty.

Black Douglas had said that beauty should not be formal, and Sabrina found that the irregular features of the house gave it an added charm; it held the eye and offered more than a stately, well-planned house.

With its rambling terraces, odd up and down staircases leading to roofs and patios, in its setting of royal palms, giant mango trees, and wild growing banana bushes, it had a sweeping view over the Caribbean towards the mountains. It had a double-gabled roof for coolness, and there were slatted jalousies at the windows giving it a secretive air. Some rooms were panelled with mahogany, where splendid unlit chandeliers dripped with crystals that stirred and tinkled in the whirring of the fans.

There were terraces paved in blue stone, verandas draped with frangipani, a pool for swimming, a squash court, and a pavilion used long ago for dances and tea parties.

Now the high-fanned chairs along the terraces were rarely used for guests, and the gardens grew tangled and wild under the tropic sun. The house stood isolated on its island, and Black Douglas seemed not to mind that it was falling into shadow as the trees grew higher and their branches interlocked, while the snake-like vines ripened in the tropic warmth and spread a net of jungle growth around Snapgates.

Ret was made impatient by this attitude of his cousin's, and Sabrina could sympathize. But Ret in his freedom from affliction should be more tolerant. He lived off his cousin's bounty, though he managed in a lazy way the coffee plantation that was still worked by the family. Their other interests had waned. The sugar canes had gone to straw, and the banana yield had tapered off since many of the islanders had drifted away to work in other lands.

This island that slumbered like a giant reptile in the coloured sea was now a blind man's retreat; a wild paradise gone to seed, a place in the sun for the remaining members of the Saint-Sarne family. Theirs had been a dynasty.

'The story of your family would make quite a book,' Sabrina said to Ret, who had been showing her the coffee hills. Now they walked down a track into the garden around the house. 'Have you any inclination towards authorship?'

She smiled as she spoke, for in every detail Ret was a true descendant of that gay and handsome buck. In his fawn shirt and white breeches, with a slouch hat shading his eyes, he should have made a fool of her heart, but she remained curiously immune to his physical appeal. She was glad of it, for she would have hated to be that pathetic figure of fun, the plain spinster in love with the dashing young plantocrat.

Sabrina quite enjoyed his company, for he always

had plenty to tell her about the Saint-Sarnes, but she was too level-headed, too deep in her shell, like a hermit crab, to be responsive to grey eyes whose bluish glint was one of mockery. She knew it would have amused Ret to flirt with her, the only English girl on the island, but she wasn't here to be hurt by a man, she was here to look after a man hurt by misfortune.

'My inclinations,' he drawled, 'are of a less academic nature. Are you so dedicated to duty that you never feel the urge to be anything but the ministering angel?'

'I've never regarded myself as an angel, only as a skilled person who contributes something towards the well-being of others. You wouldn't feel this, Mr. Saint-Sarne, being a more decorative member of society.'

'You mean that I take, like the honey-bee, while others give? Well, if you are the giving sort, Nurse Muir, what will you give me?' He stopped walking, swivelled so that he stood in her path, and made it necessary for her to stop walking. The green shadows were all about them, dappling her white nurse's dress and shading her hair to a strange ashen colour. Her eyes, always too large for her face, dwelt not with alarm but indulgence on his face.

'I learned quite young that men find me a mouse, so don't waste your talents on me,' she said.

'You arouse my curiosity, do you know that? Why don't you like men? Whatever happened to make you so armoured against their wiles? Come on! I promise not to divulge your secret to Black Douglas.'

'I think I would be more inclined to tell him my secrets!'

'Ah, is the little white mouse developing a crush on her dark and stumbling patient? I've heard that it

34

happens.'

'Not in my case,' she said firmly.

'Why not in your case? You're a woman, aren't you?'

'Yes, but—'

His eyes mocked her hesitation. 'Looking after children, and caring for a big, helpless, black-haired man, are two entirely different things. Don't forget, a man in the dark sees things differently from a man in daylight.'

She flushed painfully and went to brush past him; at once he caught her by the wrist and the action brought her in contact with his lean breeched figure. 'We're going to live under the same roof for a while, little nurse, so we might as well be friends.'

'I'm willing to be friends, Mr. Saint-Sarne.' She laid stress on the name, and at once his fingers tightened painfully against the bones of her wrist, and he studied her defiant face and the way her nape-drawn hair emphasized the size of her eyes. They dominated her other features, excluded them, so that she seemed to eat all that she looked at with their largeness.

'You could be quite fetching if you used a little make-up.' Ret tipped her chin and framed her face with his hand. 'Have you ever been kissed?'

'How dare you—?'

'It's my nature, nurse, to dare even the devil. No Saint-Sarne is excluded from a touch of arrogance and self-will. I think I shall kiss you, and then we'll see if you will look at me as if I'm a naughty boy who should have been spanked in the nursery.'

Even as he bent his head to plant a kiss on her mouth, Sabrina was driven by his audacity to laugh in his good-looking face. It was as if she had dropped a

35

grass snake down his neck. He let her go as if stung, and then a look of scorn flashed across his face.

'Who'd want you, anyway? You're just a little nobody, and a man would have to be blind to get hot under the collar for you! You know you're all set for the shelf and that's why you're touchy. No man would want to show you off as his wife!'

With these words, acid with a truth already known to Sabrina, Ret went on his way to the house, leaving her to sink back against a tree and to pluck aimlessly an orchid climbing low on the trunk. She studied it and thought how beautiful it was, golden and perfect and spattered with tiny markings. She put it against her cheek and the petals felt like velvet . . . and all at once the hot, painful tears stung her eyes. She blinked them away fiercely, for to cry over a man like Ret was to waste emotion.

All his life he had been spoiled by the admiration of other people, and he had whipped at her, finding her weak spot with the unerring aim of a man rejected by a girl for the first time . . . a plain girl who should have been flattered!

Sabrina loved beauty with all the secret passion of the plain, and it wasn't that she was heart-hurt by Ret; it was something he had said, a tip of the lash leaving a tiny wound.

'A man would have to be blind . . . blind and in the dark ever to feel desire for Sabrina Muir.'

Well, she had shown Master Ret that she wasn't to be played around with, and tucking the golden orchid in the breast pocket of her tropical uniform she followed the tracks his booted feet had left, and told herself that from now on she would be on guard against any tiny rift in her shell. Having never known affection it would be too easy to fall victim to a smile, and only she knew how sensitive she was.

She came to a side door of the house, where flame flower spread its dark fire against the white wall. The colonies of cicadas were concealed in the creepers, a low and vibrant chirring that followed her into the courtyard. There by the arched door with its curtain of thunbergia, yellow and scented, she stood very still and wondered if the man who sat smoking by the fountain had heard her entrance.

He made no sign that he had. He lifted his cigar and drew on it. With the calm hand he found the tall glass that held his drink and he carried it to his lips. To the casual observer he would have seemed like other men, able to see the beauty all around him, the clump of shasta daisies, the wicked red zinnias, and Chinese asters.

He wore a smoke-blue shirt with half sleeves, and his slacks were a pale grey. Sabrina did not stir as he sat there on the stone rim of the fountain and lifted his face to the raw gold of the sun. Only a blind man could have looked so directly at the tropic sunlight.

There was about his strong and lonely figure the appeal of something primitive, and watching him in silence, unobserved, Sabrina sensed in him the disillusion of a man who had loved and bitterly lost. He had that withdrawn quality of a man held by a broken dream . . . had the woman not been able to accept his blindness, or had he felt inadequate because he could no longer stride out into the world, the financial hawk feared by other men?

The need for love in his darkness would be more acute, and yet such was his pride that Sabrina could imagine him rejecting that love in case it turned to pity.

'Will you join me in a planter's punch, nurse?'

She was so startled when he spoke that she clenched a handful of thunbergia and the crushed petals stung the air with their aromatic scent. 'How did you know it was me?' she asked, made more curious each day by his sentient ability to feel a presence and to be nearly always correct in his guesswork.

'Because no one else in this house has your gift for total silence and stillness.'

'Be honest, sir.'

'I caught the rustle of your crisp uniform a second before you saw me and froze like a doe in a thicket with a lion.'

She laughed, yet there was an undeniable element of truth in the statement. He couldn't know that even blind he seemed more vital, more dangerous than other men. When he had his sight those radiant grey eyes would have swept over her and not seen her. But now she was part of his daily routine and they were intimately involved. A children's nurse since she had left the nursing home four years ago, she still wasn't used to having a self-willed male patient. Late last night he had rung the bell which connected with her bedroom. Dashing to him, she had found him not in pain but restless, desirous of hot coffee and a chapter from a book about sailing.

She had read to him and it had not occurred to him that she might be tired and in need of her sleep. When at last she had left him asleep in his great mahogany bed the clock in the hall had struck two sonorous notes in the silence of the great house.

Was he arrogant? For arrogance fed itself on the lonely fear of not being wanted or needed. Had she not been a nurse, then in her loneliness of spirit she might have developed a disregard for others; the same walled-in isolation. It was something she must help combat, this tendency of Douglas Saint-Sarne to become the blind recluse with servants to do his bidding.

People should be invited to the house . . . those iron gates should be thrown open and Ret's friends should come here and fill the garden and the verandas with their gaiety. It could do no harm, and perhaps she would mention to Mrs Saint-Sarne that her grandson needed worldly company; that of pretty women who would make him feel that he was not cut off from the world of laughter and love.

'Shall I shout for Nim to bring you a glass of punch, nurse?'

'I'll call the boy and ask him to bring me a glass of lime juice and ice.'

'There is ice in your voice, nurse, and I bet you're frowning. What have I done now?'

'You seem to think that every member of this household is at your beck and call. That we all revolve around you and your desires.'

'You do,' he said coolly. 'Half the time Nim is asleep under a shade tree somewhere, or he's sloping off to his shell collecting. He's supposed to stay within earshot and jump to heel when I shout for him. Just as you are.'

'Really?'

'Yes, nurse, really.' A smile flickered on the firm lips that yet had a boldness not indicative of self-denial. Despite her wish to be severe with him, Sabrina found the wish fading when she looked into the eyes that could not see her face. They were deep as mountain tarns . . . eyes that saw only darkness and could not

39

know if his smile was returned.

'I'll find Nim,' she said. 'Your glass is empty, sir. Would you like another planter's punch?'

'I rather feel as if you would like to give me a spank for my dictatorial ways. Would you, Sabrina?'

'I doubt whether it would have much effect on you,' she replied.

'Because my hide is tough, and your hand is tender? Beware, nurse! I take no pity from you or anyone else. This damn blindness is bad enough to tolerate, but I'd be even less of a man if I had to be an object of compassion. I might become so wild that I'd have to prove I am still a man . . . do you understand me?'

'Yes.' She spoke rather faintly and drew out of reach of his arms or his cane.

'Take my glass if you're going to have it refilled.'

She hesitated, and a slow, devilish smile stole over his dark face. 'Scared I shall make a grab for you in what I'm sure is a delectable white uniform?'

'Please hand me the glass, sir.'

'You little coward!' His hand made one of those deliberate movements towards the glass and as if the fingers of the blind became magnetic it was lifted and held by him without mishap. He held it out and Sabrina took it. 'Bravo!' he murmured, and she walked away from him, feeling as if he could see the girl he was building up in his mind. Slim and yet curvaceous; fair and white-clad. The sort of female who might awake the desires so sternly suppressed by him; the nurse who was often in his room, who gave him coffee in the small hours, while the rest of the household slept.

She found Nim, who was the colour of a fawn and equally long-limbed, fast asleep beneath a curtain of jacaranda. She shook him awake and told him to fetch

40

a jug of lime juice and cracked ice; to wash the master's tall glass and fetch her one like it. Black Douglas had imbibed enough island rum for one afternoon, and a dash of lime and ice might cool his imagination.

Nim dashed away to do her bidding, and after collecting her composure in the violet shadow of the jacaranda, she returned to the fountain and sat down on the other side of the stone rim, built wide for this purpose. The water ran cool in the sunlight, piped up from the sea, as was the water for the fish ponds and the swimming pool. A large stone tank on the flat roof of the kitchen served the house with fresh water; the store being fed from the sky when it rained, or brought from the mainland in barrels on board the schooner that also carried other goods required at Snapgates.

'Have you been walking with Ret, and was it interesting?' came the query from the other side of the fountain, a faintly ironic note in the deep voice.

'Yes, he showed me the coffee plantation. I never knew that coffee bushes were so attractive.'

'The berries are until the sun starts to bake them, then they are plucked, sorted and sold.'

'You do make it sound like a commercial.'

'How did Ret make it sound?'

'He related the history of the coffee trade, and I can still smell the piquant scent of the brown-gold coffee trees. This island, which Ret tells me you almost own by now, is quite a paradise, though parts of it are running wild.'

'That's the way I want it. The island and I will grow shaggy together, for I don't suppose you will always stay to see that my hair is properly combed. No nurse can abide my temper and my moods for long, unless

41

she's an angel of mercy. Are you, Sabrina?'

'You know I'm not, sir.'

'I'll send you packing on the next schooner if you don't stop calling me *sir*. I'm not in my dotage!'

'Hardly.' She cooled her wrists under the spray of water and watched the drops run down over her skin, which was beginning to take a light tan.

'Then would you kindly call me by my name? Say it ... Douglas.'

'I ... can't.' The skin of her face and neck grew warm with a strange confusion. 'You are my employer ... my patient. First names are for friendship.'

'I see. You don't feel friendly with me? You reserve that for my handsome and charming cousin. I notice you call him Ret without a qualm.'

'There must be a certain amount of formality between a nurse and her patient. Please, may I call you *m'sieur*, as Nim does?'

'Sabrina,' he groaned, 'do you think of yourself as my servant?'

'You said yourself that I am here to do your bidding.'

'Do you always take so seriously what men say?'

She could have replied that men never bothered as a rule to talk to her on equal terms, but suddenly it was exciting that she was the focus of this man's entire attention; a man who could only see the features portrayed by his mind's eye. Even apart from him on the fountain Sabrina could feel the magnetic, and lonely, and rather angry reaching out for contact with her. He thought her pretty, and though she realized the danger in allowing him to believe it, she let slip the moment when she could have said:

'I am not attractive to men, *m'sieur*. I wear my hair in

an old-maidish bun because it floats about like dandelion fluff if I don't and my cap won't sit straight. My eyes are far too big for my face, and I have no distinction at all. I haven't even the courage to buy the daring kind of clothes that make other plain girls colourful to men. I am the sort of young woman you would never have looked at had we met before you became blind.'

She said none of this, and felt the shock of being admired for the first time in her life. She took the orchid from her pocket and stared at it. Only a while ago she had sworn to stay safe and snug in her shell and now she broke that oath for the sake of being an object of interest to Black Douglas.

'Are you sulking?' he demanded. 'You must know by now that I have a sardonic sense of humour. Can't you take it?'

'I haven't been a nurse for seven years without learning how to take the rough with the smooth, *m'sieur*.'

'The French blood in our veins is a mere dash of nutmeg on the toddy by now, but call me *m'sieur* if you wish it. It sounds a bit less like master and maid!'

Nim arrived with the jug of lime juice, a gay green-gold colour, with ice floating in it straight from the icebox. Sabrina poured it out and placed the long cool glass in her patient's palm. He took a sip and she awaited his sarcasm. Instead he smiled, a twist of lip and eyebrow that was more expressive than words.

'Cool and good for me,' he drawled, 'like my nurse. The disembodied hand which offers comfort in my darkness. Yet which only touches me to feel my pulse, to fix my tie, to put into my hand the lime juice famous for its cooling effect on tropical impulses. Take heed, Sabrina. You are now in the tropics yourself and may

43

lose your own composure.'

'I am well trained, *m'sieur*.' She sat primly on the edge of the fountain and held her glass as if it were her first champagne.

'You had one of those matrons who are spartans for discipline, eh? I hope you don't intend to discipline me? Try it at your peril!'

'I'm sure it would be perilous. To tame a lion one needs a whip, and I have no such weapon in my nursing bag.'

'You have tamed Brutus to your darned seducing hand. D'you stroke him?'

'No, *m'sieur*. I play with him on the beach. I sling driftwood in the surf and he chases it. Of course, he is a duty dog and I promise not to spoil him.'

'What a charming picture the pair of you must make ... beauty and the beast.'

His words struck at Sabrina, blows in the dark, causing a pain he was unaware of. She had asked for this in not telling him flatly that she was no beauty ... she flushed painfully, for what if he had made such a remark in front of Ret! How Ret would have laughed, looking at her all the time with scornful glints in his eyes.

'I sense that you have gone as still as a bird, nurse. Aren't your patients allowed to pay compliments?'

'I ... I told you from the start, *m'sieur*. I'm quite ordinary.'

'How would I know? I can only judge from voices ... my world is one of sounds, of doors that open to admit faceless people. My darkness is absolute.' He said it with deadly calm. 'I shall never see with my eyes again, unless I wish to face death.'

A shudder ran through her, and with his sentience

44

she knew he felt it.

'They told you, didn't they? I was on a jet flight to Tel Aviv to attend a business conference. The jet was hijacked and we were held hostage in the desert. I have a temper, as you know, and I had to make a protest. One of the rebels struck me several times with the butt of his gun and I knew no more until I regained awareness in a hospital in Tel Aviv. It was a week later that I collapsed again in London; an emergency operation was performed. Those cracks over the head had fractured my skull and a sliver of bone had embedded itself in that part of the brain connected with the optic process. I became blind ... if that deeper operation is ever performed I shall die, or become what is termed a vegetable.'

Silence ... prolonged ... broken only by the persistent chorus of cicadas unseen but ever present in a tropical garden, chirring softly and madly, intoxicated by the tropic warmth.

'My grandmother told you, surely?'

'Yes, but not in such explicit terms. Is it so certain—?'

'As certain as medical science can be these days, and that's pretty close to the bone ... close enough for the truth to hurt like hell and damnation. I hate being blind, but at least I am a perceptive person ... a man still, if you have the nerve to stand me. None of the others who came here had the spirit to stand up to me.' He paused significantly. 'Only beauty can brave the devil.'

'Don't—' She spoke in a strangled voice.

'Don't call myself a devil? But I am one, Sabrina. It made me speak out when I should have held my tongue. I'd not be like this, toting a white cane, if I

45

could be tame and not the Black Douglas named for the Norman who long, long ago planted in our family the seed of fury. Most Saint-Sarnes have been fair and good to look at, like Ret. Then I was born—'

He laughèd sardonically. 'Black hair . . . black heart . . . black day and night.'

'Please, don't be bitter,' Sabrina pleaded. 'You have faculties other people lack even though they can see. You have a powerful intellect. Your travels and your success are not over.'

'They are, nurse, because I make them so! Always this island was marked out for my retirement . . . my island in the sunset of my life. Well, it came sooner than I anticipated, and I'm as content as Black Douglas could ever expect to be. I was restless, now my wings are clipped. Here if I stumble like a dolt, or fall on my face, only my family and my nurse will see it. That's how much devilish pride I have, Sabrina.'

'So you are in retreat, *m'sieur*?'

'Quite so, nurse. And having been born on this island I know it well and can visualize its beauty. The strangeness was at first not knowing day from night; night from morning. I had to listen for the birds, await the feel of the sun, the sound of the world coming alive again. In some ways it was like being born again . . . an adult baby, no less!'

Sabrina could have cried for him, but she knew she must laugh, and she did so. Pity he would despise, so she must always be his challenge.

'You think me wry, Sabrina?'

'I think you have courage . . . a big baby learning new things, with a liking for rum rather than milk. I feel rather sorry for the first nurse who had you in her charge.'

'Do you?' His smile was dry and reflective, and he gazed directly at Sabrina, using her voice as his guide. 'Would you mind if I asked you a personal thing?'

'Personal?' Her voice was hesitant, but her heart raced curiously.

'I know your voice, but I'd like to know your face. I can't see it, but if you would let me . . . it will only take a moment?'

'You mean . . . you would like to touch my face?'

'If I may. It won't be painful,' he added dryly.

Sabrina stared at him, and the moment was somehow fateful. She could refuse his request, and he would shrug and change the subject. If she allowed him to patrol her features with those lean, strong fingers he might realize her lack of beauty . . . and she might not forget so easily what it felt like to be touched by him.

'Are you afraid of me, after all?' he drawled.

'No.' With abrupt resolve she stood up and came to him; she knelt in the ferny plants clustering at the base of the fountain, and she fought not to tremble as he brailled her with his firm, sure touch. Fingering her hair and discovering its texture. Playing over the thin, sensitive planes and bones of her face. Gliding down to her slim neck, her shoulders, and pausing there with a sort of deliberation.

'What colour are your eyes?' he asked.

'A sort of brown . . .'

'And your hair is fair?'

'Yes.'

'And did it hurt to let me have my way?'

'No . . . but it isn't quite ethical. A nurse should have more control over her patient.'

His fingers came to her lips as she spoke, seeking a smile and finding a tremor. 'I forget that you have

47

been a children's nurse, and that you might find me strange . . . a moody male, difficult and demanding. You are a small girl. Your face fits into my hand . . .'

And as he spoke, there were footfalls on the paving of the courtyard. Sabrina heard them and pulled sharply away from Douglas, but not soon enough not to have been seen by Ret, kneeling there with his cousin's hand framing her face, from which every atom of colour fled. Her great eyes dwelt on Ret's amused face, pleading with him not to laugh.

'Is that you, Ret?'

'It is. I see you've been brailling Nurse Muir.'

'I wanted to find out if her face matched her unusual voice.'

'And does it?' Ret was staring at Sabrina, who was crushing slowly in her hand the gold orchid she had plucked.

'You know that better than I, Ret. You can see her.'

Ret could see her tormented face, until she turned and hurried into the house, shivering in the sudden airiness of the fan-cooled hall. She felt as if Douglas had placed her without intention in the power of his slightly unscrupulous cousin, for even a blind man would hate to learn that he had been treating a plain spinster nurse as if she were Melisande the fair!

Sabrina ran up the curving staircase to her room, and after closing the door behind her she stood with her back to it, looking and feeling a creature at bay. Her sensitivity felt stung . . . not since she was nineteen, when a patient had asked for a prettier nurse, had she felt so mortified.

Ret had looked at her with the amused scorn of someone who thought she was deliberately inviting the attention of Douglas . . . who could not see her!

CHAPTER FOUR

THERE WAS a spectacular view of the moonlit sea from the great oriel window on the gallery near Sabrina's sitting-room, and she was restless tonight. The scene was too beautiful, too beckoning for sleep, and even from here she could smell the spray and hear the soft lament of the sea.

On impulse she made for her bedroom and took from the drawer her swimsuit and a towelling wrap. She swiftly changed into the suit, then wearing the short wrap and a pair of sneakers she ran downstairs to the side door that led through the courtyard to the cliffs. From there a path sloped down to the beach.

The sea beckoned and she could not resist; the surf rippled and softly called, and she sped down the path in her eagerness to answer that call.

For too long had she been chained to city life, and bedsides. Here on this island something free and yearning had been released within her, and suddenly she paused on the pathway to pull the pins from her hair. She lifted her face to the moon and she ran to meet the sea with her windblown hair in her eyes.

Day and night the surf lapped this shore, and there was peace in the sound, and at other times a restlessness, a sort of hunger, as though the sea would sweep right over the island in order to know it, and love it.

There had never been anything much for Sabrina to love, and here the hurt was fading when she thought of her sunless childhood; her girlhood that ached for a dream to happen, while her evenings were spent with duty. She paused on the sands, thrilled by the night, and the husky whispering of the surf as it touched the sands, caressed and ran away, returned and then left bare the shells and the shingle. Sabrina kicked off her sneakers and dropped her wrap to the sands. She walked into the surf and it rippled cool over her feet and climbed to her knees as she waded out among the silvery moontrails. She knew there was an undertow, but it was out near the reef and she wouldn't swim that far. She would not believe that on such a night there could be harm in anything. Her cares were held at bay; there was no one here to spoil the enchantment.

She swam alone until she tired and waded back to the sands where her wrap lay. She drew it on and the towelling dried some of the water. Her hair hung wet and long to her shoulders, and she felt a stranger to herself as she sat there in the moonlight and the blissful exhaustion drained out of her limbs.

A person alone could not be hurt except by her thoughts, and she would think of nothing but the beauty of the tropical night, with the moon afloat on its side in that crushed-velvet sky aglow with stars.

She would not think of other girls who on such a night had someone to feel romantic about them. She filtered the fine pale sand through her fingers and heard the rustling of sand crabs in the shadows, and the sibilant murmur of the drooping palm leaves. Several days had passed since Ret had seen her being brailled by the man she now thought of as Black Douglas. Ret had not said anything – yet – and some of her embarrassment had ebbed away. After all, it was quite usual for a blind man to braille the faces he could not see . . . but not every man was quite like her patient.

She lay back on the sands and gazed up at the stars

through the palm fronds. They seemed to swing a little as the fronds waved in the soft ocean breeze, and now she had let her patient into her thoughts he would not leave them.

He was now using her to answer the letters which continued to come to him from London ... yesterday while looking in his desk for a large envelope, she had let slip from a manilla folder a batch of photographs. They had rained black and glossy to the deep carpet, and the man by the window, lounging there in his usual cloud of cigar smoke, had not been aware that she was on her knees, picking them up and looking at each one, seeing again and again the girl on his arm, emerging from a famous restaurant, smiling in a première crowd with him, stepping into a gleaming car, draped in silk and mink, lovely as only a top fashion model could be.

She was the one! Sabrina knew it instinctively, just as she knew the girl's name and her profession. Nadi Darrel, daughter of a famous jewellery designer, and darling of the fashion magazines. Courted and wooed by a train of distinguished men, all of them some years older than Nadi, and all of them rich.

It did not shock Sabrina that Douglas Saint-Sarne had loved so lovely a creature. Nor did it surprise her that when he became blind they had parted.

Nadi loved the social whirl and the glitter of flash-light bulbs; she lived for stunning clothes and admiration.

Black Douglas could no longer whirl her through the doors of international restaurants and clubs. He could no longer admire her beauty; it had become for him a memory ... and it would not occur to a girl like Nadi, who lived so much in the present, that memories could

51

take on a clarity and a poignancy far beyond the every-day encounter. Memory could be cruel, but it could also cling to what it had loved with a desperate longing, idealizing every aspect of that person.

So lost in reflection was Sabrina that she almost jumped out of her skin when a voice murmured: '*La lune, c'est belle.*'

She turned to look, and her eyes were huge in her face as they dwelt on Ret, suave in a white dinner jacket over dark trousers, his fair hair just ruffled enough to make him rakishly handsome, his sideburns slanting down towards the cleft chin. Both cousins had that cleft chin, but in Ret it was more of a dimple, a thumb-print of the gods to set off his good looks. In Douglas it was a clefting of rock, deep and shadowed by his darkness.

Ret stood above her, hands at rest in the pockets of his crisp white jacket, his polished, handmade shoes in the pale sand near her bare feet.

'All alone with the moonshine and your dreams?' His eyes flicked her hair, which hung in tendrils about her neck. 'I see you've been in the water. Do you prefer to swim alone?'

'Yes, I like to be alone.'

'You say it so convincingly, don't you?'

The scent of the ocean hung in the air, along with the burning memory of Ret discovering her with Black Douglas, his dark hand cradling her face as if it were a piece of the jade or ivory which he kept in his den. The many books he could not read; his pictures he could not see, but his antiques, collected during his business travels, he could handle and find pleasure in.

'You look different with your hair in a salty tangle instead of a schoolmarmish bun.' Ret's eyes gazed down at her and enjoyed the look in her eyes, the entreaty, and the lonely pain, veiled suddenly by her lashes. As she looked away from him, she heard him laugh softly.

'My cousin had a girl, you know. Gorgeous and brunette, with shining eyes green as dragonfly wings. She was an expensive, spoiled young darling, and when he lost his sight, she lost her nerve. But I am sure she kept the emeralds he gave her, the sable coat and the dashing Rolls convertible. She kept his heart as well, I believe.'

'Her name was Nadi Darrel,' Sabrina murmured.

'Did he tell you about her?' There was a note of surprise in Ret's voice. 'You really are infiltrating, but I suppose you've always been the type people confide in.'

'You dislike me very much, don't you, Mr. Saint-Sarne?'

'Do you mind, Sabrina?'

'No.' She spoke with total honesty. 'What is the use of minding something so inevitable, like the colour of one's eyes? All the tears in the world won't wash out a colour that one doesn't care for.'

'Tears, Sabrina?' His voice had curiously altered, had become charged with a sort of fascination. 'Are you saying that I make you want to cry . . . because of what I said the other day, after I had shown you the coffee and we stopped to talk under the orchid trees? Did I hurt you?'

'Yes, but I soon recovered.' She gazed at the sea, and saw the leap of spray over the coral reef. So lovely from here, yet so treacherous with its undertow and its lurking sharks. 'There is always some cruelty in beauty, and people like me who have no beauty are often victims of

53

the painful remark.[5]

'Sabrina—'

'Please don't bother to say you're sorry, Ret. You were being honest, and I'm no longer nineteen—'

'When something traumatic happened to you?'

'You could say that.'

'Did you fall in love and did the man break your heart?'

'I've never been in love.' She rose to her feet and looked around for her shoes ... she gave a startled cry as Ret caught hold of her and pulled her to him. Her wrap flew open and her swim-suit figure was crushed against the lean hardness of him. She lifted wild eyes to his face and saw him clearly in the moonlight, recklessly handsome, a strand of fair hair across his forehead, a glitter to his eyes.

'You sound shattered and need putting together again ... don't fight me, Sabrina. Relax, enjoy the moon-madness—'

'Leave me alone!' she gasped. 'I – I'm not some quaint sort of amusement for you, because you're bored! Take your hands off me!'

'Why, because they aren't *his* hands?' Ret gripped her sea-tangled hair and pulled her head back until she thought her neck would break. His face came down to meet hers and she twisted painfully to avoid his lips ... she wrestled with him and kicked at him with her bare feet ... he laughed ... and then stopped laughing as there came a discreet cough and a voice spoke about a yard away from them.

'Begging your pardon, Mr. Ret, but would it be convenient for the master's nurse to go to him? He's in pain, and Madam sent me to find the young lady.'

Surprised by Charles, Ret relaxed his hold on

Sabrina, who tore herself out of his arms and raced barefoot up the stepped path to the cliffs. Concern for her patient was uppermost in her mind; she could not worry about that embarrassing beach scene right now. Charles was devoted to Laura Saint-Sarne and he would be discreet ... but oh, how Sabrina would have enjoyed slapping that handsome face of Ret's! He didn't really want to make love to her ... he wanted to make her life at Snapgates so unbearable that she would leave.

He didn't like Douglas ... and Douglas had need of her!

She arrived breathless at the house and met Mrs. Saint-Sarne on the gallery. 'I'm sorry ... I've been swimming.'

'Child,' Laura gripped her arm, 'he has that awful head pain. I went in to see him before retiring and he was slumped across the bed, grinding the pillows with his hands. Please hurry—'

'Yes!' Sabrina hastened into her room, where she grabbed her nursing case without pausing to change her swimsuit. The incongruity of attending to her patient in such an outfit did not matter. He could not see her, and her entire concern was to give him the injection that would take away the pain.

When he felt her hands, touching him and easing him, he gave a small groan of relief mixed with quiet fury.

'I'm sorry I wasn't here—'

'Not your fault, Sabrina. It's the self-inadequacy I hate! The man groping along a tunnel of black pain and not being able to help himself ... ah, now your big baby feels better! You are very skilful, nurse. You make the needle feel like a love bite.'

'Please – relax, sir.'

'Sir?' His smile was tired and quizzical.

She smiled a little herself and smoothed his damp black hair away from his eyes. His face against the pillows was drawn, the lines etched deep but smoothing out as the pain lost its edge. As she leaned over him to make him comfortable, she was more acutely aware of her state of undress than she had been with Ret. She saw the proud nostrils expand as he took a deep breath.

'I can smell the sea on you, nurse.'

'I've been down to have a moonlight swim, that's why I wasn't here when you rang your bell. I am sorry . . .'

'Is the moon shining tonight? I didn't ring the bell . . . I tried to fight it out on my own, and then Nan came in and saw me.'

'Douglas, dear?' Laura came to his bedside, desperately concerned, her lovely chiffon robe floating around her. She was a mixture of sugar and steel in her daily dealings with people and the running of the house, but she became helpless when these attacks of pain plunged her grandson into nerve-torn loneliness and torment. 'Are you now all right, dear boy? Is the pain going away?'

'I'm fine, Grand'mère. You mustn't worry so.'

Sabrina smiled reassuringly at Laura and made her escape into her own bedroom, where she quickly discarded her swim-wear and put on a pair of pyjamas and a quilted robe. It was late but she would sit with her patient for a while, until he fell asleep.

She shivered as she combed her hair and pinned it up again. Her neck still ached from Ret's rough treatment . . . and her heart still ached for Black Douglas.

A nurse had no right to become so involved with a patient, but never before had she dealt with anyone so big, so vital, and yet so terribly at the mercy of the darkness.

Her big baby!

She stared at her own face in the mirror. At the age of nineteen, which was a romantic age, she had felt the trauma of being unwanted by a patient because she wasn't pretty ... but what would Ret Saint-Sarne do if he ever found out about the other trauma in her life ... the one which had sent her running out of England like a hare with the hounds after her?

Tightening the sash about her robe, and stiffening her spine, she returned to her patient's bedroom. With tact and firmness she finally persuaded Laura to go to bed. She wasn't a young woman, although it was hard to think of her as close on seventy. With her piled white hair, soft and shining, and her fine, cared-for skin, she had an ageless attraction. She had the true Saint-Sarne good looks, for she had been a cousin of the man she had married. It was she who had told Sabrina that Douglas was a throwback to the Norman line running in the family veins. He was like the ancestor who had carried off a bride and locked her in his castle. Terrified of him, because he had such a reputation for swordsmanship and hawking, she had climbed out on a battlement, and had sat there in the moonlight crying, too frightened to make a move. That other Black Douglas had risked his six-foot weight on the old stone wall and had carried her back into the castle. The legend went that for her he had put away his sword for a year, until his son was born and his young bride passed away.

'The dark Saint-Sarnes are cursed in our family,'

Laura had said. 'They never find lasting happiness. There was another who in the Great War was injured on the Flanders battlefield. He had married while on leave ... when he returned home badly disfigured the girl ran screaming from his bedside.'

'Good night, Sabrina.' Laura stood on the gallery and gazed about her with troubled eyes. 'Sometimes in the night like this I feel as if this old house were dying. Things creak, and lizards leave marks in the dust. The timbers grow more sun-faded, and the trees creep closer up the drive. Once it was a happy house. I can remember the cane harvesting, and the islanders toting the great hands of bananas to the boats. I loved it here as a girl ... long-gone days you will never see, my dear.'

'Someone should write the history of Snapgates, Mrs. Saint-Sarne.'

'Douglas could do it ... he could dictate into one of those tape-recorders.' Laura drew a sigh. 'He could, but he won't. He broods over that girl ... good night, take care of him!'

'I shall. Good night, Mrs. Saint-Sarne.'

Soon the purple wrap had floated out of sight and a door closed at the far end of the gallery. A lizard clung still as a stone to a picture frame and its tiny eyes seemed to stare at Sabrina. It was a house of memories, with a master who would not marry because the girl he loved was not the kind who could devote herself to a blind man.

Sabrina semi-darkened the room, from habit, and took her patient's pulse. It had returned almost to normal, and the colour had crept back into his face. 'How are you feeling now, *m'sieur*?' she asked quietly.

'As if I float on a cloud, and you can't imagine how

odd it feels, Sabrina. Like being on a carousel without lights, and swinging in a void.' Suddenly he clutched her hand and clung to it in his darkness that was so impenetrable. 'When I sleep I have dreams, and I see in them, do you know that? I see faces I have known. It's in dreams that I love ... that I *live*. A slip of the tongue, nurse!'

'Freudian?' she murmured, and he would never know that her smile was sad for him, sad for herself.

'You really are a most intelligent young creature. Why the devil are you still free and footloose? Are all the seeing men blind?'

'I'm a career girl.' The smile twisted off her mouth, and she almost lost her professional composure. 'Go to sleep, *m'sieur*. In the morning you will feel much better, and the sun will be shining to warm you.'

'All my bruises eased, nurse? My aches and fears alleviated for a while?'

'Things always seem more significant at night, *m'sieur*.'

'My night without stars or moon, nurse? My blackness without a glimpse of your white uniform of mercy?' His hand moved its position and found her bare arm under the sleeve of her robe. 'Ah, you see how I confuse the hours! I am forgetting that it must be very late and you are tired yourself. I am a selfish brute!'

'No! It's my job to look after you when you suffer. I came to Snapgates for that very purpose.'

'And do you like the house whose gates snap shut on the world outside them? Is it reassuring to be cut off from the clamour of life on an island?'

'I think it is.' As she spoke she tried not to think of Ret and his embrace. 'Most people dream of a palm island, warm seas and coconut trees. I feel very glad that your grandmother accepted my application.'

'Why did you apply?'

As she tautened she felt the tightening of his fingers about her arm. 'I wanted and needed a change—'

'Would you have come if you had known that your patient would be a blind man . . . arrogant to boot!'

'Arrogant from head to heel,' she laughed.

'Added to which the occasional big-daddy spider creeps into your bath, and there are the everlasting kickers.'

'I don't mind the cicadas and their tropical calypso.'

'Discretion is the better part of nursing, eh? You also have nice skin.' His fingers slid down her arm and left their warmth on her skin. 'I think I shall sleep now — au 'voir.'

She gazed down at him as his lashes settled, curtaining the grey eyes that could not see her as she allowed herself a long look at his dark features. As he fell asleep he looked almost serene, and on the hand that had held her there was the gleam of a ring on his small finger. A black-stoned signet ring. The hand itself was strong and yet not coarse, with the shadow of dark hair curling from the sleeve of his pyjama jacket.

'Sleep, and dream of *her* if you must, Black Douglas.' And with these whispered words Sabrina took the armchair that stood near the bed and sat there for about an hour, listening to her patient's steady breathing, and the tiny creaks of the furniture settling after the warmth of the day.

So often in the past had she sat like this, but with a fretful child instead of a man who had made her feel sad when he had said: 'In dreams I see . . . I live . . .

I love.'

When she left him to go to bed he didn't stir. He was deeply asleep, one arm flung across the covers as if he held there, in his dreams, the lovely Nadi Darrel.

Whatever the outcome of her post on the Coloured Lake, Sabrina made up her mind to enjoy all that the island offered. She might stay only a short time, who could tell? But during that time she would savour its delights and hoard them against rainy days in England.

Her patient's powers of recovery were allied to his strong physique and when he was free of pain he ordered his car brought out from the garage and informed Sabrina that she could drive him into town, which was fifteen miles from Snapgates.

The car had an open top and was black with deep red upholstery. Laura came out of the house to ensure that her grandson was comfortably settled in the seat beside his nurse. 'Take care of him!' she mouthed at Sabrina, but he knew instantly what was passing from one woman to the other.

'Don't fuss, Nan!' he growled.

'You have ears like a hawk!' Laura exclaimed.

'I need some kind of protection against the female instinct for smothering, so stop acting as if I'm in diapers instead of blinkers, Nan, and I shall be duly appreciative.'

His grandmother was always Nan when he was feeling self-willed and impatient of his blindness, and the look she gave Sabrina was a rather helpless one. Laura wanted to keep him safe, with no stumbling stones in his path, no dangers that he could not leap clear of because he could not see them. She meant well,

Sabrina knew, but this man must be encouraged to face the world.

'It's all right, Mrs. Saint-Sarne,' she said soothingly. 'I'm really quite a good driver, and the island roads are wonderfully free of traffic and offer none of the hazards of city driving.'

'Quite so,' he said decisively. 'I am going to see my bank manager and to do some shopping, then Nurse Muir will lunch with me. She will also drive at the pace I tell her to.'

'Douglas, you really are a brute when you feel like it!' Laura leaned over and kissed him before he realized her intention. 'Don't bully the girl or she'll drive off the road into something. Sabrina, do try to ignore his instructions and don't let him flurry you. He gets pleasure out of that.'

'I'm quite sure he does,' Sabrina said demurely, and when she looked at him his jaw was set and his hands were gripping the cane that was the white symbol of his darkness. Once he would have driven as recklessly as Ret around this island, a girl his passenger instead of his driver. 'Are you ready, *m'sieur?*'

'I can't wait, nurse! Will you buy me a candy-ball, and a bucket and spade to play with?'

'Douglas!'

'It's all right, Mrs. Saint-Sarne. I'm getting used to his sarcasm. It's a sign that he's feeling fit and full of himself.'

He smiled grimly as the engine sprang to life beneath her touch. 'You had better beware then, nurse. Is she looking pretty, Nan? All in pink perhaps, with her blonde hair shining round her neck?'

Laura glanced rather curiously at Sabrina, who was wearing a doeskin skirt and a soft white shirt, with her hair in its usual orderly style. 'Good-bye, madam,' Sabrina said hastily. 'I promise to drive carefully.'

'Good-bye, child. And behave yourself, boy!'

'I'm past the age, Grand'mère,' he said wickedly.

Laura waved, though he couldn't see her, and the Studebaker Avanti drove away smoothly from the house and under the vaulting of the flame trees that lined the drive to the gates. Petals fell like pieces of fire, spattering the car like mock confetti. Douglas must have felt them, and one or two were clinging to his impeccable white seersucker when they paused for the gates to be opened by Josh, who grinned amiably at Sabrina.

'Mornin', boss. You got a day sweet as cream for drivin'.'

'Yes indeed, Josh. How are Janie and the children?'

'Right fine, boss. Ah got five chillun now.'

'That's a nice handful. My regards to the missus.'

'Sure thing, Mr. Douglas.' Josh flashed his white teeth as the car turned out of the gates.

'The flame trees must be looking at their loveliest,' said the man at Sabrina's side. 'Each wedding day of a Saint-Sarne a flame tree is planted along that avenue. Unless Ret marries there will not be another planted.'

'It seems a pity,' Sabrina murmured. 'There should be a tree for the master of Snapgates.'

'The master without a mate,' he drawled. 'No, we don't break traditions in our family, and if there isn't a bride to cover the roots with the first spadeful of Saint-Sarne soil, then there will be no tree, no branches smothered in passion flowers. Black Douglas won't be a burden on any woman ... and don't tell me, nurse, that I'm just like other men!'

'I wasn't going to tell you any such thing.'

'Oh?'

'You aren't like other men, unless you have a twin soul around.'

'Smart, aren't you?'

'Merely logical, *m'sieur.*'

'Leave logic to tailors and bankers, Sabrina. It doesn't suit a pretty girl.'

'Please—' She was about to beg him not to call her pretty when she noticed a fallen tree in the path of the car and drove around it. Gay-hued birds flew about in the foliage at either side of the road, and the occasional monkey could be seen swinging about. It was a gorgeous day, and suddenly Sabrina didn't want to spoil it in any way for her patient. Let him think that she was everything he liked in a girl, gay and smart, and attractive to men. Let him believe that other men would look at her and envy him for being with her.

'You drive well,' he said. 'Who taught you?'

'A professional driving instructor. It was something I thought would be useful in my work as a private nurse. I had a small car of my own back in England.'

'Why did you really leave England?'

'I told you, *m'sieur.*'

'You said you felt like a change of climate ... one day you might tell me why your voice holds a note of tension whenever I mention England. I no longer have the sight of a hawk, but you heard what Nan said about my hearing.'

She cast a quick look at his profile and thought that he looked hawkish; dark, strongly sculptured, life-bitten. The white seersucker sat without a wrinkle on his wide shoulders, and his bow tie was perfectly straight. He had allowed Charles to fuss over him today. His black hair was well groomed, and he was too close-shaven to have shaved himself with his safety razor.

Sabrina knew it was foolish of her, but today she made no attempt to fight the attraction he had for her as a man. Today she didn't want to think of him as her patient. She wanted for a few stolen hours to be treated as if she were Nadi Darrel.

CHAPTER FIVE

SABRINA parked the car near the old slave market, which was teeming this morning with a gay assortment of island folk. Their faces were as warm-coloured as rum, and their rich laughter mingled with their bargaining over the piles of tropical fruit and vegetables, and the vivid displays of fish, both in the shell and out of it.

'I'll rest my hand on your arm and you will guide me to the bank.' As Black Douglas spoke he sought Sabrina's arm. 'If we're standing near the old slave block you should see the bank just across the road.'

'Yes, *m'sieur.*' She guided him through the crowd to the colonnaded bank that must be almost as old as the port itself. The sloops and trading boats still came laden with goods, and there were a few painted dhows moored by the wharf, giving an impression of the wild old days, when chains had held the wrists and ankles of these jovial people. Now the men sauntered about in sea-cotton shirts, and the torsos of the sailors unloading the boats gleamed like bronze. Their songs were gay and rhythmic, and the clink of earrings had replaced the sound of chains.

Black Douglas took a deep breath of the spicy air. 'The scene is one to dazzle the eyes, isn't it, Sabrina?'

'Yes, it's like a vivid painting on a huge canvas ... be careful, *m'sieur*, there are steps!'

'There are always steps,' he growled, but he mounted them without stumbling and his fingers gripped her wrist as if to impart his satisfaction with himself for not

66

making it obvious to everyone that he was a blind man dependent on a girl.

Cool ceiling fans whirled inside the bank. He was expected, for a clerk came forward to take him to the manager's office. Sabrina waited in the foyer and gazed through the windows at the passing crowd. Market day on the island was like a fiesta, and she smiled irresistibly. She must take note of everything, hoard each moment, each colourful cameo, for one day in less exciting surroundings she would have need of her memories.

She turned with a start when the bank clerk came to her side. 'Mr. Saint-Sarne wishes you to come to the manager's office, miss. Your advice on a certain matter is desired.'

'My advice?' She looked puzzled as she followed him to the office that was tucked away in a niche of the building, panelled, with London prints on the walls, and looking very much as it must have looked in the heyday of the sugar and rum kings.

Her patient was seated in a leather chair at one side of the lion-footed desk, and the manager introduced himself as Mr. Warren and drew forward a chair for Sabrina. She sat down and noticed at once the black vault box that stood open in front of Douglas Saint-Sarne.

'Nurse Muir is in my confidence,' he said to Mr. Warren. 'She knows that as I shall never marry these family gems will be of no future use to me, and I can see no reason for letting them remain in the vault when they can be put to use elsewhere.'

He turned his head and found Sabrina by the catch of her breath. He seemed to stare right at her, his gaze so direct beneath the dark gable of his brows. 'What I want, Sabrina, is for you to choose a necklace and brooch for my grandmother, and a piece of jewellery, pretty and suitable for a girl of your own age. The remainder will be sold to aid an organization for the relief of orphaned children, of which I am a member.'

Sabrina gazed speechlessly at him, and saw from the obstinate set of his chin, with its deep shadowed cleft, that he had made up his mind to take this step. Some of the jewellery must have been in his family for years and to discard it was a sign that he felt hopeless about the future. She wanted to argue with him ... to say outright that not all women were as self-interested as Nadi Darrel, and that he was still a man to be loved for himself. Love was a sharing of misfortune, and if right now he felt cut adrift from love because of Nadi's desertion, it wasn't to say that he would always be alone. A voice might speak out of the darkness, and a hand might touch him to which he would thrill again, then he would regret his decision to sell the jewels that his bride had every right to wear ... especially these pearls, which ran like milk through Sabrina's fingers.

'Go on,' he spoke impatiently. 'Make the selection, then we will leave Mr. Warren to arrange the sale of the remainder. Nurse, don't be sentimental about jewels! They don't mean much when a man can't see them adorning the woman he might have married.'

'Very well, Mr. Saint-Sarne. There's a treble string of pearls which I feel sure your grandmother would love, and a pearl and sapphire brooch. Would you like to handle them ... the pearls are graduated and quite glorious. I – I don't think they should go out of your family.'

'Let me feel.' He took the pearls from her hand and

lifted them a moment against his dark cheek. 'Like silk, eh? Yes, they will suit Nan, and the sapphires will match her eyes. Now that other piece ... for a young woman.'

Sabrina cast a rather helpless glance at his adamant face, then she bent over the box and took from it a velvet, shell-shaped box. She opened it and could not help but love what it contained, an exquisite jade shell on a fine gold chain.

'I – I think any girl would like this,' she said, and she placed it in his hand so that he might braille it with his fingers. He did so for about a minute, then he sought her hand and pressed the charm and chain deep in her palm.

'You keep it,' he said brusquely. 'Are there any diamonds in the box ... I seem to remember a pair of diamond drop earrings.'

Confused that he should give her the shell and chain, not quite sure she ought to accept it, Sabrina found the diamond earrings, and she knew for whom they were intended. They would look perfect swinging against a cloud of brunette hair!

'Well, have you found the earrings?' he demanded.

'Yes, Mr. Saint-Sarne.'

'Very well,' she saw his mouth twist sarcastically, 'Nurse Muir. If you have a handbag put the things in it, and then we will leave Mr. Warren to his business.'

'You are absolutely certain you wish me to dispose of the remaining jewels?' Mr. Warren looked a trifle worried as he gazed at his blind client. 'The disposition will be easy, of course, but—'

'There are no buts,' said Black Douglas decisively.

'You know where to send the cheque, Mr. Warren. It should keep quite a few young bellies well fed for a year or so. Childish hunger is better catered for than female vanity. And now, nurse, we'll be on our way!'

They bade the manager goodbye and proceeded out of the bank. Sabrina was aware of the eyes upon them as they passed the counters on the way to the doors. She caught the glances of curiosity and pity, and was fiercely glad that Black Douglas was unaware of them ... and then a foolish woman had to speak, and his ears were too keen not to catch what she said:

'How simply awful to see Douglas Saint-Sarne like that! He was always such a leader of people ... now to see him led about!'

Sabrina felt the hard, angry tremor that raked through his body. 'Get me out of here!' he muttered. 'Hurry ... before I tell that darn woman to take her pity to hell!'

Out in the open and above the steps, Sabrina gripped his sleeve for a steadying moment. 'Please ... she isn't worth a fall.'

'You too, nurse? Pitying the poor blind oaf!'

'You know how I feel! You're about as helpless as a grumpy lion, but onlookers just don't understand. Now watch your temper, *m'sieur,* and we'll navigate these steps without any trouble at all.'

His hand pressed her arm painfully, and she accepted the pain he inflicted on her with a sort of blitheness. He might adore Nadi Darrel with a blind, hopeless passion, but he needed Sabrina Muir. She was his thin, young, spirited shield against the women who stared at him with pitying eyes, and shrank away from his biting, blundering touch. She would have bruises on her arm tomorrow, but it wouldn't matter, because suddenly she knew how much she loved him.

They were at the foot of the steps and she steered him into the shade of a side street. 'Where do we go now, *m'sieur*? You said you wanted to go shopping—'

'Charles can see to that – I want a drink, nurse! A long, cool gin, ice and tonic. Are we in a snaky little street to the left of the the bank?'

'Yes—'

'Then let's keep walking. Somewhere along here there's a place called Bellefonda's.'

'Hideaway, *m'sieur*?'

'What do you mean by that?'

'You know what I mean. You're afraid someone else will say something about your blindness.'

'Damn you, Muir!'

'Yes, *m'sieur*. Damn me for speaking the truth.'

'When I want the truth I'll ask for it. You just do your job and do as you're told. Come on!'

'You said we would lunch at the famous Colony Club. I looked forward to lunching on the gallery where the Princess sat.'

'A snob, as well?'

'Anything you like to call me. A nurse gets used to being called names.'

'Don't pacify me, either. I'm not one of your infants.'

'You're behaving like one. Does it really matter so much that a foolish woman felt a bit sorry for you? If you had a broken leg you wouldn't mind a little sympathy.'

'Stop arguing and let's go to the darn Colony Club. I suppose I owe you a decent lunch for letting me snarl at you.' Suddenly his touch was intolerably gentle, finding her slender shoulder under the thin material of

71

her shirt. They stood locked in silence in that side street, shut off from the crowded market, and she heard the breath catch in his throat. She was unafraid as she saw the grey eyes blaze and darken. She felt in him the fierce, lonely hunger for the girl who could have made his blindness so much more bearable.

His fingers touched her throat. 'You aren't wearing the shell and chain, nurse. Don't you like it?'

'Of course—'

'Then put it on. A shell is the symbol of protectiveness and you need something of the sort around that slim young neck when I start on you. You're all soft skin and bird bones, Muir. Don't you eat enough?'

'I eat sufficient for my size, *m'sieu*.' Her hands were trembling with the reaction of being touched by him in such an intimate way, and she fumbled with the catch of the gold chain as she fastened it around her neck. The jade shell fitted into the hollow of her throat, and never in her life had she been given so pretty a gift by anyone . . . least of all a man.

'Have you put it on?'

'Yes, *m'sieur*. It's so generous of you to give it to me. I shall take great care of it. Thank you.'

'You'll have earned far more than that by the time we part! Now we will go and feed you up at the Colony. We go round by the market place and along the main avenue with its royal palms. The club is all white stone, verandas, and large showy hibiscus . . . as I remember it.'

She steered him without too much jostling through the market place, and all about them were shoppers, and women in broad-brimmed hats selling strange things like queen conch and guava cheese. Head

72

baskets were laden with yams, bunches of plantains, and lobsters still stretching their claws. At the heart of the crowd beat the compulsive rhythm of a calypso.

Black Douglas walked through it all in darkness, his hand resting upon Sabrina's wrist, his fingers tensile and brown against her pale skin. When they reached the avenue there were fewer people to jostle him, and the air was cooled by the waving fronds of the handsome palm trees that lined this road leading up to the colonial club, with its flower-hung verandas overlooking the sea.

They were shown to a table shaded by orange trumpet vine and out of sight of the other diners. The menu was handed to Sabrina. 'Choose something you've never had,' Black Douglas said to her.

Love, she thought. 'Oysters,' she said.

'Hoping to find a pearl?'

'That would be nice.'

'Quite. Even a man can appreciate a pearl. We will both have the oysters,' he said to the waiter. 'And afterwards Steak Diane if it's on the menu. With a green salad and golden fried potatoes ... my nurse doesn't need to watch the calories.'

When they were served and left alone, Sabrina watched anxiously as her companion ate his oysters off the shell ... he could so easily stab his lip with the fork.

'Baby Douglas won't spill sauce all down his nice white suit, nurse!'

'Don't be absurd.' She had to laugh. 'I can never imagine you as a baby, anyway.'

'Well, I can assure you I didn't arrive in this world needing to shave twice a day. I've been thinking lately of growing a beard. It would save myself and

73

Charles a tiresome job. Do you think a beard would suit me?'

'You'd look villainous, *m'sieur.*'

'Thank you so much for the compliment!'

'You are so very dark.'

'My name means "dark water". Nan told me that directly my mother saw me she said there was only one name for me, Douglas. She was a French girl whom my father met when he was shot down over France during the war. She escaped with him to Dover and they were married in a half-bombed chapel. All very romantic, eh? Yet I'm glad she didn't live to see my sight plunged into darkness. I was an only child and she made rather a lot of me after my father was killed towards the end of the war.'

'Then we are both orphans,' Sabrina murmured, and try as she might she couldn't picture him as a child. He had such power and strength as he sat there in the sunlight, and his blindness seemed only an illusion when his grey eyes dwelt on her face, directed by her voice. Apollyon, she thought, angel of the blackness.

'Have you been much alone, Sabrina?' he asked, his fingers seeking his wine glass and carrying it to his lips, his eyes never leaving her face, as if he could see her . . . the pretty blonde nurse of his imagination.

'Nurses are always in demand, *m'sieur.* There is always someone who needs to be cared for.'

'I am talking . . . I suppose I am asking about the men in your life, and it's extremely discourteous of me. This steak really is delicious. You are enjoying it?'

'Very much, *m'sieur.* I'm grateful to you for bringing me here.'

'Are you looking at the sea? I can hear that persistent whispering of the surf . . . we must go swimming some time.'

'Do you – ?'

'Yes,' he said dryly. 'For me the water is safer than a street. No traffic except the occasional shark, and when you can't see the fin and the long jaw full of teeth you don't worry about it. Sharks are funny creatures. I've often swum in our private bay and they must often have been about, but they seem to take me for one of them. Maybe because my darkness alleviates the panic that can arise from seeing the object of one's fear ... or even the object of one's desire.'

'You have developed senses, *m'sieur*, that make you unafraid of the things I would fear. Nature is never entirely cruel. She compensates.'

'Does a course in wisdom go with the training to be a nurse?'

'To be a good nurse one needs to be under-standing.'

'And you feel you understand me?'

'In as far as you will allow of it. I realize that to be blinded makes for bitterness, and as you were never a sweet and docile person at the start, you can't be ex-pected to behave like a perfect angel now.'

'And you consider that you cope with the black angel?'

'I won't be browbeaten. I know you despise a lack of spirit.'

'Do you care that I have preferences when it comes to women?'

'All men have those, I imagine, but it wouldn't do for a kitten to be leading a lion. One snap of your teeth and I'd be howling.'

'I might yet make you cry.' His teeth were bared for an instant in a half-savage smile. 'You have large eyes, haven't you, Muir? Wise and sometimes a tiny bit wicked. With you I can be honest. I sense that you also have been through a traumatic experience, but I'm not going to ask questions. I hate people who pry. Now what shall we have for dessert? Waiter!'

They had spiced peaches with *crême* Chantilly, ice-cool. And far below them shimmered a dozen sea tints of blue, lizard, topaz and gold. The waiter topped up their coffee cups, holding twin silver pots and pouring coffee and hot milk together.

For Sabrina this lunch had been memorable.

It wasn't until they left the Colony Club and were making their way along the harbour where the yacht basin was situated that the day took on a significance that was acute.

The air was spiced with ginger bush and seaweed; ocean salt and coral. A yacht had just come in, sea blue and white, its sails still unfurled. A girl was standing at the rail with her brunette hair blowing in the sea wind. She wore a lime-coloured halter and pencil-slim trousers, and the colours were striking against her tanned skin. Her eyes as they swept the waterfront were a shining, metallic green.

Sabrina stumbled as she noticed the girl, and it was Black Douglas who gripped her arm and steadied her. 'Watch your step, nurse,' he drawled.

Sabrina was watching the girl on the yacht . . . Nadi Darrel . . . arriving out of the blue on this island where Douglas Saint-Sarne sought to forget her!

There flashed through Sabrina a fierce desire to protect him from this beautiful and heartless girl who for some reason of her own had come back into his life. Sabrina led him down a side lane, out of sight of the yacht. He could not see Nadi, but she might see him, and he was unprepared for a meeting with her.

A meeting that was inevitable.

They drove home at a steady pace, and the afternoon was somnolent after the activity they left behind them. Sabrina compared Nadi's arrival with her own. That day the harbour had been deserted, with rain in the air. She had been brought to the island in a cockleshell boat with a brave little rag of a sail, and there had been no one waiting for her.

'You've gone very quiet, Sabrina.' Black Douglas sat smoking a thin cigar, the aromatic smoke blowing across her nostrils, brushing her cheek, imparting a sense of intimacy that now felt unbearably threatened.

'Of what are you thinking?' he persisted.

'That I've grown fond of this your lotus island, *m'sieur.*'

'Of course, but don't say it like someone who expects soon to say goodbye to it. I am not displeased with you, nurse. You suit me quite well ... don't I suit you?'

'Yes ... but life has a way of altering from one day to the next. It's a mistake to become too fond of places.'

'And of people, eh?' A thread of cynicism ran through the words.

'People are even more dangerous,' she agreed.

'Are you thinking of anyone in particular? Ah, there I go again, probing into your secrets, thinking I can get away with it because I'm blind and can't see if you look annoyed or embarrassed. It's a bad habit, but the trouble is that the senses grow very keen when a person cannot see, and I sense a change of mood in you since we left the club and the harbour.'

'I'm concentrating on my driving, *m'sieur.*' She

forced herself to speak lightly, though a tiny nerve tugged at her lip. 'The sun is in my eyes and I forgot my smoked glasses.'

'I understand.' He spoke dryly. 'It wouldn't do for both of us to drive blindly. I imagine the sun is burning down through the trees. I can remember that sudden dazzle, then the shadow, following one upon the other. It can bewilder a driver.'

He was agreeing with her, and yet she knew that he was curious about her. The relationship between them had undergone a subtle change since he had shared with her the disposition of the family jewels and given her something that had once belonged to a Saint-Sarne bride. They were no longer just patient and nurse. He had opened one of the secret doors of himself and allowed her inside ... therefore he was going to demand the same of her; he was going to take possession of her secrets, her loneliness, her longing to mean something to someone. He was going to do all this without dreaming that it would affect her emotionally.

She wanted to beg him to be distant with her ... and yet something inside her was crying out that he do whatever he willed with her. That she was there to make less intolerable his blindness.

She was the hand held out to him in the darkness. The whipping boy when he had hurtful things to say. The intriguing key to a mystery. He had need of her, if not desire, and she knew that her role was not to be a shadow of the desirable creature who had left him with indelible memories of her gaiety and charm.

Sabrina's role was to keep him safe, and to care for him because he was someone dear and dangerous and special. She mustn't wish again to be treated as anything but his plain and devoted nurse. No one must ever know how much pleasure and pain she garnered from just being with Black Douglas.

She drove along with more assurance, and wasn't conscious that she had straightened her spine, and tilted her chin until he spoke thoughtfully beside her:

'You made a decision just then . . . I felt it distinctly. Were you thinking of leaving me to the uncertain mercy of yet another nurse and have you changed your mind?'

'Yes, m'sieur.'

'Why consider leaving? Do you find children less demanding, after all?'

She could have replied that she found them less dangerous, but her decision to stay was made, and she was about to assure him of this when the car suddenly lost speed and slowed down to a halt. She gazed unbelievingly at the petrol gauge . . . it had fallen to nil.

'Have we paused to admire the view?' her passenger drawled.

'No – I'm afraid we've run out of gas.'

'You don't say?' Suddenly a deep rumble of laughter came from his throat. 'I've heard of it happening, but it's usually in reverse, with the girl at the mercy of the situation.'

'I am an idiot! We were so busy talking to your grandmother this morning that I forgot to check on the gauge.'

'The tank is usually full, but I expect Ret has had the car out. He has his own, but what is mine seems to attract him. Describe exactly where we are and I shall be able to judge whether or not we have a long walk home.'

'To the right of us there is forest all tangled over with wild pink hibiscus and vine, to the left a jutting out of

79

the road above the sea. We've stalled on the incline that rises gradually to the cliffs.'

'Which means a nice stiff walk in the heat . . . unless we go down to the shore and follow the beach until we arrive below the cliffs and mount the steps to the back of Snapgates. It's quite a distance, but cooler by the water than panting uphill . . . out of the car, Sabrina, and see if there's a way down!'

'But—'

'I'm not totally helpless, nurse! Do you fancy a flogging walk all the way up Sheba Hill?'

'No – no, of course not.' She did his bidding and slipped out of the car. She went among the trees to the edge of the incline and saw a rough path wending its way down to the shore, where the turbulent surf beat the stones and filled the air with its torn-silk rustling. Coconut trees waved their fronds and they were the only occupants of that long and lonely stretch of beach.

Sabrina studied the path to the beach and saw that it was overgrown but a gradual slope rather than a sheer one. If she went ahead of her patient and guided him out of the way of the larger clumps of wild flower and root, then they should manage all right. A walk along the beach was certainly preferable to a climb up the twisting hill to the bluff on which Snapgates was situated.

She returned to the car and explained about the path.

'Good. It should take about an hour to reach the bay and we'll be in time to see the sun go down. At least,' he added dryly, 'you will see it. I can remember it. Like other pictures it's clear and vivid in my mind, at dawn and dusk.'

He sought his way out of the car and Sabrina restrained herself from helping him. This had been the hardest lesson to learn; never to assist him unless it was absolutely vital. The eager, reaching hand could sometimes be more hindrance than help to a blind person, and Black Douglas was by nature an independent man.

'Lock the car, nurse. Charles can arrange to have it taken home later on. Are we all set?'

'Yes, *m'sieur*.'

'Then lead on, Sabrina.'

CHAPTER SIX

SABRINA glanced back and saw outlined by the setting
sun their footprints in the sea-wet sands, a chain of
large and small foot carvings along the shore, slowly
dissolving as the surf rippled in. Far out the spume
above the coral reef had turned pink, and she could
hear the boom of the sea as it battered the chains of
coral.

Black Douglas paused on the sands and gazed
towards the sound of the waves. 'The sea is merciless,
primitive, almost attuned to the emotion of love. Listen
to that deep, dark music, Sabrina. It speaks of many
things, so boundless and eternal, like the heart of man
that is battered one moment, caressed the next.'

Sabrina breathed the sea and the mystery into
her very being, and she heard the music in the waves, a
low throbbing rising to a rhythmic thunder, as if shark-
skin drums were being pounded by passionate fingers.

'Is the sunset very beautiful?' he asked.

'How do you know the sun is setting, *m'sieur*?'

'Because I can't feel its touch on my face. Are you
looking at the sun, falling like a golden ball into the
water?'

'I am,' she said, but she had no need to look at the
sunset, it was in his eyes burning there and yet leaving
them as dark as the day would become when the quick
tropical dusk fell. It always amazed her how quickly
everything went dark, with no gradual falling of the
veils as in England.

'We should be moving, *m'sieur*. Soon it will be dark

and—'

'And then I shall lead you, Sabrina. The night is my companion, the sounds are more distinct and I can follow them like tiny signals. Do you hear the crabs scurrying in the powdered coral? They forage for food and do their courting in the dark. Do you know, nurse, it makes a change to be able to talk like this to someone. I never used to in the old days. There was always too much to do ... the people I knew then would not understand the man I have become since I must use my ears instead of my eyes.'

He fell silent and made marks in the sand with the ferrule of his cane. 'The beauty of a speaking voice now has more meaning than the beauty of a face. So must it be. I am now a judge of footfalls, and of perfume. I imagine you, nurse, rather like a water-deer, both shy and daring; graceful and sometimes awkward. Your perfume is very discreet, and I'm sure your mode of dress is very chaste ... and your desires in chains.' As he spoke he moved and was suddenly close to her. She had not been expecting him to do this, or to say what he had said, and she backed from him and gave a little gasp as she found herself against the trunk of a palm tree.

'You sound ... chaste,' he drawled. 'Are you afraid of a blind man? If you ran I couldn't catch you, and I'm sure you are as fleet as the water-deer. Are you crying?' His hand groped for her face. 'What a foolish child you are to let me upset you!'

'You said it yourself, *m'sieur*.' She felt stifled by the silly tears, and his strong, unknowing, dark and vital nearness. 'People don't pity you when you hurt them.'

'It hurts you that I speak of your desires? Where did you leave them? In England – ah yes, I said I wouldn't ask, but when a girl like you comes to Snapgates out of the blue I have to know why. You are the best nurse I've had, but if some man is likely to call you back to him, then I really must be told.'

'Does it always have to be a man?' She fought back the tears as she had learned to. 'I could have stolen something, or given the wrong drug, or made an enemy.'

'All three would be out of character, nurse.'

'Do you feel you know me that well, *m'sieur*?'

'*Touché*,' he drawled. 'I suppose I am in the dark about you, in more ways than one. When I think of Nan, or Ret, or any of the people I knew before the curtain came down I still judge from remembrance of the face.' His fingers brailled again the contours and bones of her face, and again she held her breath. His touch was against her lips, sliding upwards to her cheekbones, and to her eyes. She closed her lids and his darkness was hers as he traced with his fingertips the outlines of her eyes.

'What an extraordinary size your eyes are, Sabrina.'

'All the better to see my patients with,' she said lightly, but inwardly she was trembling. She knew what he was leading up to . . . his curiosity was such that only by kissing her would he know that she was entirely untouched by any man. That never had there been made upon her the physical demands of a love affair. It was what he suspected, but it was quite untrue. She had not left England because of a man.

Fearing his kiss with a hundred fears, she tensed against the rough woven bark of the palm tree and hoped he would release her. But he didn't. His hands gripped her upper arms and she felt the quickening of his breathing.

'Don't – please!'

'Isn't it ethical . . . or isn't it desired?'

She felt the throbbing of her pulses, in tune with the primeval throb of the sea caressing roughly the coral that was a living, breathing thing.

'You're just curious about me, and I have the right not to like this form of investigation. It isn't fair, because you are stronger than I am, because you pay my salary a—and give me a neck chain to wear!'

His hands found her neck and the jade charm in the hollow of her throat. His fingers against her skin were an exquisite torture. She wanted to be touched and held by him, but it was something she couldn't have, not from Black Douglas, who didn't yet know that the girl who was the substance of his dreams was here on the island!

'I – I didn't know when I accepted the jade and chain that I should be expected to pay for them.'

The words were said . . . there was no recalling them . . . and then with brutal retaliation he made her cry out as he caught her to him and crushed breath and resistance from her slim body. As her cry opened her lips he took them, and his kiss was deliberate and quite relentless. In the darkness he was the master. In his embrace she felt all the pain he had suffered, and her yielding was not entirely forced from her.

When he let her go the surf was around their feet and the sea was like ebony against the pale glint of the beach. The palm fronds rustled and night had fallen around them.

'Thank you,' he drawled. 'I wonder what I'd get for diamonds?'

His kiss had ripped open the heavens for her . . . his

words plunged her into despair.

'Shall we go home?' she asked.

'Is there anywhere else to go?'

She bit her lip, and then noticed that his cane had fallen to the sands. She picked it up and placed the curved handle over his arm.

'Putting me in my place, nurse?'

'W-what do you mean, sir?'

'A blind man is not a very desirable object, is he?' With these words he began to walk ahead of her, and when they reached the steps that had been cut in the cliffside it was Sabrina who stumbled in the dark.

'This really is a case of the blind leading the blind,' he drawled. 'Perhaps we should have waited for the moon to rise.'

'It might be a good idea to have these steps wired for lights,' she said. 'The tropics always seem that much darker ... I suppose in comparison to the brilliance of the sun.'

'As I recall the moon always had a more vital glow in this part of the world. Did you notice when you swam in it the other night?'

It had been a half-moon surfing among the stars, she remembered. A pagan and romantic moon. 'It was golden,' she murmured.

'The exact shade of champagne, eh?'

'I wouldn't know ... I've never had champagne.'

'Poor, deprived wench! I suppose it was a struggling young doctor you were enamoured of ... it usually is. Good-looking and dedicated—'

'Please stop it, *m'sieur*!'

'Can't you bear to talk about your traumatic experience?'

'No more than you can bear to ask about Nadi

Darrel!' Again ... oh, dear heaven, once again he had driven her to reckless words beyond recall.

They had reached the bluff and he stood there like a statue, while the cicadas filled the night with their chirring, and the stars began to bloom above the heads of the mango trees. A breeze rattled the pods called woman's tongue, a tree that grew wild with the banana bush and sea-grape along the cliff edge.

'Who's been talking to you about Nadi?' he grated. 'How do you know about her?'

'I – I saw her photograph in your desk. I know of course that she's a famous model.'

'We were going to be married, did you know that? She was with me the day they told me it was lights out, and curtains, if I had the operation.' A rough emotionalism came into his voice as he stood there with his blind eyes staring at the stars they could not see, each in its perfection polishing its own small piece of heaven. 'No man wants to die, just like that! Just like a snapping of a twig.'

'Like the cutting down of a tree,' Sabrina said quietly, and her face had the pallor of a night flower as she stood beside him ... the wind on the shore had blown her hair free of its pins, and it clouded softly about her thin young face with eyes too large for her other features. Hers was a face Renoir might have painted, but she didn't know. Dashing young doctors had found her plain and dedicated. Male patients had not found her the sort they could flirt with. Only children had ever loved her.

'Was I wrong, Sabrina, to choose life in preference to death, for the sake of a woman?'

'I think you were right,' she said. 'And it's wrong for anyone to say, "I love you, but only if you can see me."'

That is self-love.'

'She's a lovely creature, Sabrina. All life and laughter 　　　 it would have been unfair, disastrous, if I had insisted she stay with me.'

'Did she make the offer, *m'sieur?*'

He shrugged and swung his cane at the nearby rattling trees. 'I would have kept her for a while, then I should have started to suspect her of looking at other men. When you can't see, you develop distrust in people, and she is not the sort for life on an island with a blind man. I can no longer be the man she fell in love with. I can't skipper my own boat, play polo at Montego Bay, or escort her to a fashion ball. I can't surf-ride or play tennis. Suddenly we – we had nothing in common except—'

He broke off and took a deep breath. 'I have my hungers, Sabrina. Men are made up of them ... a hunger for position, for money, for food ... and love. I'm no saint, but I wouldn't drag any woman through a blind life with me, least of all Nadi. If she came to the island tomorrow ... what is it, Sabrina? You gave a stifled cry. Did my cane hit you? I have a habit of chopping the air with it.'

'No ... it was a big moth,' she lied. 'It startled me.'

'They fly about like ghosts, don't they? Come, we had better go and have dinner. You must be starving after that long walk.'

She walked with him in a kind of daze, still a little unbelieving that he should talk to her of the girl whose beauty clung to his senses and haunted his dreams, made all the more desirable because never would Nadi change for him. She would always be as he had last seen her, probably at the airport the day he had flown off on his fateful business trip. Nadi would have been wearing something startling, such as only a model could wear. And her perfume would not have been discreet . . . or her desires in chains, that day.

What would happen . . . what would he do when he learned that Nadi was here on the island?

Sabrina was so busy with her thoughts that she didn't notice he had walked off the path to the house and was taking a blind, zigzag course across the garden. Before she could call out or reach him in time, he had blundered into a mass of roses and briars growing around the entrance to the unused squash court.

The long, spiked suckers whipped at him and clutched his clothing, like live things awaiting a victim, and the shock of their sting made him yell out. 'Damnation . . . what am I in? Sabrina . . . ?'

'Please stand still!' Her own hands were stabbed and bleeding as she unbuttoned his jacket and ordered him to back away from the trap formed by the wild roses. Then she tugged his jacket free and could not suppress a cry of her own as a sucker lashed at her cheek and left a painful scratch.

'The roses, eh?' He could smell their cruel and beguiling scent. 'I wondered what the devil had got hold of me! Those briars sting like hornets . . . are you all right?'

'Yes.' He wasn't to know that blood was trickling down her cheek as she led him back to the path and into the safety of the house. 'You must have those hands bathed, *m'sieur*.'

'D'you see how easy it is?' he groaned. 'One false step and I'm in trouble.'

'It was my fault,' she soothed him. 'I should have

made sure you kept to the path.'

'It's no one's fault . . . it's the darned irony of fate that I'm like this. Helpless!'

'You're far from helpless . . .'

'Let me go!' He flung off her arm. 'Call Charles and he'll attend to the scratches. I've had enough of being nursed!'

Sabrina flinched as if stung again, then she walked to the bellpull and summoned Charles. Brutus came padding out from the den and was dividing his attention between his master and Sabrina when Laura appeared in the hall. She was smiling as she came towards them, but when she saw Sabrina's scratched face, and her grandson's torn hands, she looked appalled.

'Oh, whatever happened? Have you had an accident in the car?'

'Nan!' Her grandson set his jaw and looked a trifle grim. 'Now don't fuss or I shall swear. I walked into some rose briars, like the sightless fool I am, and Sabrina plucked me out again. The scratches probably look worse than they are.'

'But Sabrina's poor face!'

'What?'

Sabrina shook a quick head at Laura, but it was too late.

'My dear child, another fraction of an inch and your eye would have been struck. How on earth did the pair of you get tangled up in rose briars? What were you doing?'

'I was making violent love to the girl!' And before Sabrina could move he had grasped her wrist, sought his way to her shoulder, and found her face. 'Little idiot, you should have yelled for one of the boys to disentangle me. You must hurt like the devil! My skin is less soft!'

'It was my job to see that you came to no harm, Mr. Saint-Sarne.' She spoke formally, and even coldly. Not by the flicker of an eyelash must she betray to his grandmother that he had kissed her with violence; that to protect him she would have leapt into a hornets' nest. She pulled away from him. 'Here is Charles. Perhaps he could bathe your hands, sir, while I attend to my own scratches.'

'Yes – Nan, perhaps you would go with Sabrina?'

'No, I shall be all right.' Sabrina made quickly for the stairs and ran up to the gallery upon which her rooms were situated. When at last she closed her door and was alone, she felt a sudden exhaustion sweep over her. What a day it had been, and now she desperately needed a long, lazy soak in a bath, easing out the sting of the briar scratches, and the combined ache of that long walk and being held so crushingly in the arms of Black Douglas.

As her cheeks took slow fire, the wound below her left eye began to throb painfully. He had kissed her with the hunger of a man long denied such close contact with a woman. She knew that for him there had been nothing personal in it, beyond gratification of the moment, and he must never know that for her his kiss had been heaven.

Alone in her bedroom with its cool beauty, so unlike other rooms in which she had slept, she could admit that she loved him and let the wonderment of it sweep over her. She loved Black Douglas with all her starved and sensitive heart; she felt a new tingling awareness of herself and everything around her. It was as if nothing had been real or meaningful until her meeting with him. He was not a patient man, or a very gentle one. There were aspects to his personality which thrilled her with fear; depths untrodden, unknown, to a girl whose heart had been untouched. Often he rampaged against his blindness, but he also faced its many obstacles with a tenacious courage.

It was going to be a struggle, a challenge to her wit and her spirit not to betray her feelings ... especially now Nadi Darrel had arrived on the island. The girl meant to see him! She meant to torment him all over again! Sabrina knew it with every one of her heightened senses, and there might be no way to shield him from that meeting, for girls like Nadi had a gift for getting their own way.

Water gushed into the deep sunken tub and while she waited for the tub to fill she bathed her cheek and applied antiseptic. The claw of the briar hardly added to her lack of beauty, and she pulled a wry face at her reflection, and as she knotted her hair she compared herself to the glamorous figure on the blue and white yacht; a girl with the cool arrogance of someone who had the world at her feet.

There flashed though Sabrina the cruel relief that Black Douglas could not see *her*. He had been concerned about her scratched face ... he would surely be scornful if a miracle should happen and he saw the real Sabrina Muir. A thin creature without style or magic. The sort who got lost in a crowd, whose hair was a pale fawn colour and so fine it looked untidy unless she pinned it into a nape knot.

Nadi's hair was rich to the eye, and no doubt abundant to the touch, and her green eyes flashed like the dragonfly wings of Ret's description. Ret! Sabrina paused on the brink of stepping into her bath, and the jade charm glinted green against the paleness of her skin. How well did he know the girl his cousin had planned to marry? His way of describing her eyes was rather poetic, and he certainly had an eye for the girls . . . not to mention a penchant for the possessions of Black Douglas.

Sabrina slid into the warm scented water and absently soaped her body. There were mirrors around the walls, but she hardly noticed herself in them. She was imagining Ret with Nadi, and in her mind's eye they were a perfect match, he so fair, the girl so dark; he so good-looking and the girl so stunning.

Nadi liked to be admired or she wouldn't be a model, which was said to be sheer hard work, and Ret had not a thing wrong with his grey eyes in which a flirtatious blue flame shimmered.

Sabrina couldn't help but feel curious . . . and fiercely protective towards her patient. He had borne enough without being hurt all over again by Nadi and the tricks she was capable of playing when it came to men and what she wanted from them. The glossy magazines had always been avidly interested in Nadi and her conquests . . . was Ret Saint-Sarne the latest?

Ret, who lived a free and easy life at his cousin's expense?

The water flew from Sabrina's heels as she stepped from her bath and towelled herself. She glowed with an inner sort of anger, and still wrapped in the big orange towel she entered her bedroom. She had forgotten to take fresh lingerie into the bathroom and was selecting a white slip and panties from her bureau when someone tapped upon her door.

'Please come in.' She turned, clutching the towel like a toga, and was sure this was Lucille, the smiling brown girl who usually brought coffee to her. The door opened and retreat was too late as Ret Saint-Sarne strolled into her room.

He was dressed to go out for the evening, with a cummerbund showing beneath the immaculate one-button fastening of his white tuxedo. The ruffle of his shirt was white as his teeth as they flashed in a smile . . . instantly gone as his gaze settled on the jade charm in the hollow of Sabrina's throat. She had not removed the charm and chain since fastening it at the behest of Black Douglas. She intended never to remove it since his fingers had caressed it down on the beach; the charm touching her skin held his touch.

'What do you want?' She clutched her lingerie and backed towards the door of the bathroom. 'I – I was just dressing.'

'You look strangely more fetching undressed.' He closed the bedroom door behind him and they were alone together. His gaze had left the jade and was fixed upon her cheek, with its cruel mark of the briar. 'I heard you went into town with Black Douglas. What has he been doing to you? Biting you?'

'Don't be ridiculous—'

'Is it so ridiculous. You're young and he's blind, and no member of this family was ever a saint, despite our name. And I see you're wearing an item of the family jewels! There's a portrait on the bend of the gallery of a Saint-Sarne bride wearing that exact chain and pendant with a low-cut period gown. It's an heirloom!'

He took a step towards her as he spoke, as if he meant to take the chain from her neck. She raised a quick hand to protect it, then realized how very inadequately clad she was. Hurriedly she pulled the orange towel more tightly round her, then she fled into the bathroom and bolted the door. She hastily dressed herself and when she was ready she stood a moment in front of the mirror, staring in to her own wide eyes, a hand clasped over the jade charm.

It wasn't for Ret to lay claim to Saint-Sarne property, not while Black Douglas lived. Snapgates and its possessions were his to keep or give away, and she was certain that the money earned by him before his blindness had gone to support the house and its occupants, and made it possible for the family jewels to remain unsold.

She pictured Ret's fury when he learned that his cousin had arranged to have most of them disposed of and the proceeds used to help orphaned children.

The few remaining items were in her handbag and she quickly re-entered her bedroom, where Ret was standing by the bureau and casually studying the photograph of a small boy which stood with her few cosmetic jars and a small silver box of hairpins.

'Nice child,' Ret drawled. 'One of your patients, I presume, as you said you had no family?'

'He was a patient of mine.' As she spoke she noticed that her bag, a soft one, lay crumpled on the bed. Temper and a sense of intrusion flared through her and angry words trembled on her lips. She wanted to snatch up her bag, which she had left tidily on the bedside table, but the action would be too obvious. Instead she asked him in a cool voice what he wanted.

He lounged against the bureau and studied her neat, almost prim appearance now she had discarded the orange towel for a plain white dress, freshly laundered by Lucille and left airing in the bathroom. Upon the right lapel hung a small watch, and with her hair drawn back at the nape of her neck she looked every inch the efficient young nurse.

'You are a deceptive person, aren't you, Sabrina?'

'I don't know exactly what you mean,' she said, but she knew well enough. He had seen the jewel cases in her bag and he had jumped to the conclusion that she was enticing jewellery out of his cousin. The idea was amusing, especially when she pictured herself in those glittering drop earrings.

'You look so cool and starched and dipped in icing, but I don't believe you're like that at all. I believe there's a lot more to you than meets the eye. I daresay you're too good to be true!' He quirked an eyebrow and looked mockingly handsome in the tropic evening wear that suited him so much. He was no doubt going into town to dine and dance, and Sabrina couldn't help but wonder if he were dining with Nadi Darrel.

'You will say what you like, Mr. Saint-Sarne, whether I like it or not.'

'How formal you are tonight! I wish you wouldn't be, for twice I've seen you very informally dressed and my pulses were not unmoved. You should buy a poppy-coloured kimono. With your skin—'

'Please stop it!' She spoke tormentedly, for unlike Douglas he could see how plain and undesirable she was, and he was taunting her, hurting her because he believed his cousin found her 'fair and pleasant' as the romantic poets wrote of it in the sonnets she read in secret. 'I am well aware of my nondescript looks, so you can stop wasting your sarcasm.'

'Don't tell me you don't enjoy being thought attractive by Black Douglas? He's been seduced by that Irish witch's voice of yours ... has he seduced you yet?'

'How dare you!'

'Holding out for a proposal of marriage?'

'You must be out of your mind!' She snatched up her bag and made for the door. She jerked it open and was out on the gallery when Ret caught her by the shoulders and swung her to face him. He was so close to her that she breathed the Tiger Balm on his shaven cheeks, and saw the tiny flames leaping in his eyes.

'I say it again, little nurse, you don't fool me with your innocent airs. From the moment you met my cousin and realized he couldn't see you, you set out to make yourself the devoted companion and cup bearer. But where did you come from? What are you running away from? You might as well tell me because I can always write to the nursing authorities in London and get the facts from them. I can always tell them I am concerned for my blind and vulnerable cousin, who should be in the hands of a trustworthy person.'

'You would really do it, wouldn't you?' she gasped, feeling the pressure of the iron balustrade as he held her to it, forcibly, while the sheer drop to the marble hall loomed beneath her slight figure, helpless in the hands of a man who played tough games such as polo. He knew her to be helpless and his eyes were exultant as they gazed down into hers . . . so might he look, handsome and devilish, a moment before he made wild love to a girl. But love was not on his mind right now, only hate, turning his fingertips to implements of torture as he gripped her, and could so easily have thrown her over the scrolled iron.

'Yes, I'd write off about you tomorrow morning.'

'Why not tonight?'

'Because tonight I have a date with a girl who makes you look a mousey nun . . . only you aren't a saintly little creature, are you? Those great big eyes of yours are hungry for the good things of life ... including love. You're so desperate that you'd accept the love of a man who has to judge by a voice. I'll grant that you have quite a pleasing voice, Sabrina. The sort for lulling kiddies off to sleep ... and wooing a man who is at the mercy of the lonely darkness.'

'As if you care about that!' Her eyes blazed, like those of a trapped fawn making a brave fight of it. 'You'd like to be the master of Snapgates, but you can't be, not while your cousin lives, and he's a strong man and isn't likely to die for a long time.'

'You call it living, to be always in the dark? How long can he hold out, stumbling around with a cane in one hand, and a dog or a nurse leading him about the island? You never knew him before it happened! He could be in two places at once, a business consultant feared and respected on four continents. Why d'you think they called him Black Douglas? Because of that rough black hair, nurse? Because the women thought him picturesque? No, he was never the great lover, but when it came to sorting out financial tangles he had something of the black arts about him. He was like Merlin to the courts of kings of commerce. He had power, nurse. Now he broods on this island, shackled to a blind man's cane. He's ready to grab at anything that will light up his darkness for a while ... and passion can do it, for a while.'

'I wouldn't dream ... oh, let me go!' She beat at Ret's shoulders and struggled for her release, and as she did so her handbag suddenly fell from her hand and dropped through an ornamental opening in the balustrade. It fell all the way to the marble flags of the hall and there it spilled its contents ... the catch of the earring case flying open and sending the diamond drops like bright tears across the floor.

'Quite a little hoard of loot, nurse!'

'They aren't mine!' The words broke in desperation from her. 'Mr. Saint-Sarne asked me to look after them. They're for Nadi, not me! I know the earrings are for her . . . but he doesn't know that she's here . . . on the island!'

Ret was still holding her and staring at her when a dark figure emerged below from the shadows of one of the arcades into which the hall was divided. He stood there, gazing upwards, his quick ears having caught the sound of voices and the words carried to him by the desperation of Sabrina to vindicate herself from Ret's accusation.

'Sabrina?' The deep voice echoed . . . thundered through her, like a crack of doom. 'Will you come down here and repeat to me what you have just said to Ret? Yes, I know you're with him!'

Ret released her and, white-faced, she walked down the stairs to where Black Douglas stood waiting for her. Ret leaned on the balustrade and watched her approach his cousin; his features were tense and sculptured in contrast to the shadowing of Douglas's by the black, frowning brows.

Sabrina was miserably aware of the drama of the moment . . . a few steps more and she would reach him and the tentative companionship they had found together would be over . . . he would ask about Nadi, whom he loved, and he would be wild that she was here, and yet the desire to hear her speak, to touch her again, would smoulder in his blind grey eyes.

CHAPTER SEVEN

'It's true, *m'sieur*.' Sabrina stood there facing him, while the contents of her bag still lay scattered about their feet. 'I saw Miss Darrel arrive by yacht . . . it was after we left the Colony and were walking back to where I had parked the car.'

'And why didn't you tell me?' Still he frowned and looked unbearably stern, his knuckles and the briar marks on his hand standing out as he gripped the handle of his cane.

'I – I didn't think it was any of my business, *m'sieur*.'

'On the contrary, you were being over-cautious. You thought I'd be excited, and it isn't good for the patient, is it? How did she look? What was she wearing? Something improbable and delightful, eh?'

'Yes. She looked even more stunning in reality than in photographs.'

'And you took it upon yourself not to say a word! That was officious of you, nurse, and a trifle too careful of my feelings! I'm not a child to be guarded from the playthings that might hurt me. The pain of the second time around is never as bad as the first time. The scar is numb, nurse, and you should know that.' He turned as if to walk away and his foot struck one of the pendant earrings. 'What was that?'

'I – I dropped my bag, sir. Everything came out.'

'Then pick the things up, girl! Don't just stand there!'

She knelt and gathered up the items and was acutely

aware of his dark, towering figure, and the irritated tap of his cane against the marble floor. The earrings felt like ice in her fingers, and her fingers shook a little as she placed the gems in the velvet case and fastened it.

Above on the gallery was the white blur of Ret's jacket. She didn't look at him, but she knew he was smiling, enjoying her humiliation at the hands of his cousin.

Well, if the scene had convinced him that she meant absolutely nothing to Black Douglas, then it had not been suffered in vain.

'Is everything salvaged?' drawled her patient.

'Yes, sir.'

'Then bring the things to the den and I'll put them away in the safe.' He preceded her the length of the hall with that uncanny precision that was rarely faulted in and around the familiar precincts of the house. He had only blundered in the garden because his mind had been on the girl he could not forget. The girl who had actually wished him to undergo the operation which could take away his life!

Love was strange . . . a kind of self-sacrifice, because no matter how deeply you were hurt, or humiliated, you remained a victim of the love you felt. So ran Sabrina's thoughts as she followed him.

He swept open the double doors and stood aside for her to enter. The lamps were aglow, because despite his blindness he never sat in darkness. Sabrina walked into the room, caressing swiftly with her eyes each detail of it; allowing her glance to linger on the portrait that hung between the long windows. Beneath it on a small polished table stood a bronze replica of a Japanese temple, its curving tier of tiny gables exquisite in their detail. He knew each antique on its separate shelf or table, and for him each one had become a link with the past, when he had been able to enjoy beauty with his eyes.

Her hands caressed the wings of his chair, just as she had seen him caress those lovely rare objects, so they took on a curious, living quality when he held them in his hands that had a strong, dark beauty of their own.

Without being handsome, he had about him a touch of primitive splendour to which Ret could never attain. The set of his head, the awesome clarity of his unseeing eyes, the deep timbre of his voice, these were part of what Sabrina loved, with a thrilled sort of hunger and delight and pain that no one ... not a soul but herself would ever know about.

Secret was her love ... her thoughts, her touch upon the chair where his dark head had rested.

He made his way to the safe, which was situated behind a sliding panel. When he had opened it, he held out his hand for the jewel cases. 'Was Ret being curious?' he asked. 'Did he imagine I had been rewarding you for services not in the nursing manual?'

'Something like that.' She was curiously gratified that Black Douglas did not braille the contents of the cases before locking them away. Before closing the safe he took from it a small, cream-white object which had the shape of a book. From its soft, old lustre, and the way he held it, she guessed it to be very valuable.

'This is Chinese,' he said. 'A rare, white jade tablet with words carved on it ... a sort of talisman. Run your fingers over it. There, it feels alive, soft yet firm, like the touch of a young woman. Strange are the things a lonely man grows to love, eh?'

'What do the words mean?' she asked. 'Each one is

like a picture.'

'So is life, that we sow a little sorrow, reap a little joy. Dream and hope. Pray and weep. So is love, that it be a tyranny best avoided, and yet unavoidable. So is death, that we sleep and the heart is still.'

'How very beautiful!' she sighed.

'It's the story of life, Sabrina.'

She placed the white jade in his hand and he locked it away, as if only now and again could he bear to let it remind him of his own sorrow, his own dreams and hopes, and the tyranny of loving someone who couldn't bear his blindness.

With his cane hooked upon his arm he opened his watch to touch the braille face of it with his fingertips. 'We have time for a glass of wine before the dinner gong. Cognac, I think. We both deserve it after getting mauled by those briars. A moment, though, before you pour it out. Did you take care of your own wounds? From the way Nan spoke you were badly scratched.'

'It hardly shows—' She was about to move away in the direction of the drinks cabinet when he caught unexpectedly at her wrist. He knew her height instinctively now and could easily find her face. It was all she could do not to tremble as he touched her cheek.

'Is this the side you were hurt?'

'Yes, sir.'

'For heaven's sake! Are we back to "master and maid" because I lost my temper with you? I had every right to know about Nadi.' Suddenly, roughly, and almost as if he could see the place, he bent his head and his lips pressed her clawed skin. 'Antiseptic,' he drawled. 'I bet you're looking all prim and starched because I do this, but it was a brave thing to do, to leap into the briars after your patient. Whatever would you do if I walked into the fire?'

'The same, I expect.' She pulled gently free of him and walked over to pour the drinks. She felt shaky and rather in need of a tot of brandy.

'Do the duties of a nurse extend to self-sacrifice?' he asked dryly. 'Or are you dedicated beyond the call of duty?'

'I – I just don't like to see people being hurt, *m'sieur.*'

'Ah, that's better! And now we're at the crux of it, aren't we? You have a soft heart, Sabrina. Sometimes it can be a burden to its owner rather than a blessing, and that heart of yours took a knock in England. It suffered a bruise, and I'd rather like to get my hands on the brute who did it.'

'Oh – why?' The expensive brandy decanter nearly dropped out of her hand, her heart very nearly stopped.

'Because I never had a young sister, I suppose. She'd have taken after my mother and been like you, kind-hearted, quick to help, and foolishly gallant. You take a devilish long time to pour a drink! More used to pouring medicine, eh?'

'Yes.' She smiled a little as she came to him, the glasses cupped in the palms of her hands. His devoted cupbearer, but never his sister! 'Here you are, *m'sieur.*' She placed one of the glasses in his palm, and her up-raised eyes dwelt with pained love on his face.

'You poured some for yourself, nurse?'

'Yes.' She let her glass clink softly against his. 'Good health!'

'Its price is above rubies, eh? Good health to you, Sabrina, and next time I walk into trouble don't risk your skin or your neck to rescue me ... that's an order!'

She flinched from the curt note in his voice and buried her nose in her brandy bowl. It seemed that always his flashes of tenderness had to be counter-balanced by a show of hardness. His nature had undergone a blow when Nadi had rejected his blindness, and only by being cruel after kindness could he retain his isolation from involvement with anyone else.

He stared at nothing as he drank his brandy. His face had taken on the stillness of a mask. He was mysterious, remote, and inaccessible to her as a person. He was only her patient.

There was a tap on the door and Charles entered the room. 'Madam has sent me to tell you that dinner is about to be served, Mr. Douglas.'

'Right you are, Charles.'

They went together to the dining-room, and all through the meal he spoke of casual things, and not once did he mention to his grandmother that Nadi Darrel was here on the island. His eyes were blank, so his thoughts were not revealed, but the very fact that he concealed what must be uppermost in his mind was a giveaway to Sabrina.

Towards the end of the meal she decided that something must be done to take his mind off his tormenting thoughts, and during coffee in the lounge she sorted through his records and loaded the radiogram with Caribbean music and songs.

When he relaxed against the velvet headrest of his chair and let his lids sink down over his eyes in a restful attitude, Sabrina breathed a sigh of relief. Tension was bad for him; it could bring on one of those devastating headaches and leave him exhausted for hours. Music was balm to the nerves, especially the soft, deep, sensuous voice of Sherry Brown, a girl from the island who had become an international singing star through Douglas Saint-Sarne's sponsorship.

Sabrina sat in a chair out of range of Laura's eyes, and unashamedly she watched her patient, wreathed in the cigar smoke that drifted from his nostrils to tangle in the black roughness of his hair.

He was a man whose love must be a tremendous emotion, yet he had given that love to a shallow young model whose main aim in life was the wearing of attractive clothes and attracting men.

Yes, love was indeed strange when such a man could lose head and heart to someone so unworthy of him ... and Sabrina didn't care if the expression was an old-fashioned one. Love itself was as old as the story of Eden.

The rhythm of drums died softly away and there was silence in the long, cool room. The records had played themselves out, and moonlight was flooding across the veranda near where Sabrina sat. The ghost moths darted in and out of the shadows, and the night air was filled with a hundred scents of island flowers.

'That was good,' Black Douglas murmured. 'I needed some repose after our rather hectic day. I have something to tell you, Grand'mère.'

'I am listening, dear boy.' Laura glanced up from her crossword puzzle. 'But first do give me a five-letter word for the three faces under one hood. Curiouser and curiouser, as Alice would say.'

Her grandson gave his sardonic laugh. 'I think you'll find it's a flower. The viola, so delicate and yet so brave.'

'Viola! Let me see ... oh, you are clever, Douglas!

That fits perfectly with envoy. My dear, who do you take after for brains? Your father cared only about flying . . . you must be a throwback.'

'I'm sure I am,' he drawled. 'Now will you attend to me and I'll tell you something important that happened today?'

'I'm listening, dear. Sabrina will tell you I'm all attention.'

Sabrina had risen to her feet. 'I'll go to bed now,' she said. 'I am sure you would both like to talk in private, and I'm feeling a bit sleepy after all that island air.'

'Of course, my dear. You run along and get a good night's rest. Your eyes are looking too big for your face.'

'I'm afraid today I've been a bit more of a worry for you, nurse.' The sardonic note had deepened in her patient's voice. 'You really must try and be less objective about those in your charge. Too much dedication isn't good for a young woman, and tomorrow I'll arrange for the tennis courts to be cleared of briars and weeds, and the swimming pool can be cleaned and refilled. It's safer than our bay waters, with that undertow and the chance of foraging sharks.'

He paused and turned his head as if seeking her presence. 'You will be able to play tennis with Ret. If you can't play already, then I'm sure he'll be delighted to teach you. Well, Sabrina? No comments to make?'

'It will be nice,' she said, 'to be able to swim without having to worry about the sharks.'

He laughed again, deep and quietly in his throat. 'Good night, nurse. Sweet dreams.'

'Thank you, sir,' she replied demurely. 'Good night, Mrs. Saint-Sarne!'

On her way to bed Sabrina paused on the gallery bend and studied the portrait of the girl bride wearing the same chain and charm that she now wore. Her fingers touched it beneath the fastening of her dress, and it seemed so strange, and even made her feel a little guilty, that she should be wearing something so closely connected with this family. The girl in the portrait was primly pretty, with a breakable young neck rising out of the soft, low neckline of her dress, and the jade rested in the selfsame hollow of her throat.

Sabrina looked into the pictured eyes and they seemed to hold a tiny hint of apprehension, as if her Saint-Sarne bridegroom had been watching while she was painted, a tall, dark replica of Black Douglas, perhaps.

With almost silent footsteps Sabrina continued on her way to her bedroom. She had said she was sleepy, but in reality she was restless and she wandered out on to the balcony and sat down in a cane-backed chair.

The night was so still and lovely, as if even the cicadas were too tranced by the moon to disturb the peace. The sea barely whispered, as if it lay under the same spell.

It had not been for her that Black Douglas had decided to have put to use again the recreational amenities of Snapgates. He knew that Nadi would come to see him, and he wanted to give her some of the things that might keep her near to him. Sabrina could understand that deep, secret need of his . . . she only wished that for his sake the girl was more sincere, more attuned to the loneliness and helplessness he felt at times. He had now been blind for about seven months and it would take very much longer for him to accept the changes it had wrought in his being and his life.

He needed to be loved, with warmth, sympathy, and passion, but Sabrina knew just from looking at Nadi Darrel that she loved only one person and that was herself.

With a sigh Sabrina arose from her chair and went to bed.

Black Douglas was a man of his word and within a day a team of islanders were busy around the courts and the pool, singing as they worked in the sun, their torsos bared, their skins as warm-coloured as jungle coffee.

As the tiles of the pool were gradually cleaned they emerged as aqua blue, and the wrought-iron surround was cleared of the wild growing vines. It was an old-fashioned pool but extremely attractive, and it was Laura who told Sabrina that the pool had been a wedding gift from her husband to the portrayed girl on the gallery.

'The tale goes that he was much older than she. It's in the family records that he ...' Laura made an expressive gesture with her hands, as if to excuse and yet indulge the man, 'he won her in a card game.'

'You're kidding me!' Sabrina exclaimed.

'No, I do assure you. Men were like that in those days ... some still are ... and it truly is a fact that the girl's father was an incurable gambler and that Paul Saint-Sarne hoped to teach him a lesson by saying he'd take no I.O.U. He'd take only his daughter. That same evening the girl arrived at Snapgates complete with her trunk, and instead of sending her home again, Paul sent for the minister the very next day and they were married in the drawing-room by special licence. He had been a confirmed bachelor for years, but something about Clarice must have appealed to him. She wasn't a raving beauty, but it could have been her youth he liked, and the fact that he thought her father a worse sort of reprobate than himself. From all accounts he was remarkably good to her and she never lacked for anything. He died when she was only thirty; she never remarried but devoted her life to their son and daughter.'

'It's a romantic story,' Sabrina smiled.

'And being a modern young miss you are sceptical of it, eh?' Laura spoke as dryly as her grandson would have done. 'Although, looking at you, Sabrina, I should have thought you the type of girl to believe in a romantic love resulting from the most unlikely circumstance.'

'Why, because I'm plain and can only dream of being swept off my feet by a bold man?'

'Your face is unremarkable, but you have your attributes, Sabrina, so don't be so quick to belittle yourself. Why have you never tried wearing bolder colours?'

'Because I'm a nurse.'

'Only when you're on duty. Certain deep shades, such as jewel red or beryl, would suit that pale clear skin of yours, not to mention your eyes. They are Renoir eyes and should be flattered by dashing colours rather than the beige and the washed-out blue you are inclined to wear. If you want a husband, my child, then you'll never find one in such drab plumage. If you don't mind that I speak frankly?'

'I'm sure that like your grandson you believe in speaking your mind.' Sabrina spoke in her most demure voice. 'But I'm not exactly panting for a man. I do have quite a satisfying career, and I like working here.'

'I'm glad of that. There are times when Douglas can be trying, but you don't allow him to bully you. He reduced some of your predecessors to tantrums and tears.'

'I'm used to handling spoilt children.' Sabrina added sugar to her second cup of mid-morning coffee, and this gave her an excuse not to look directly at Laura. She had shrewd eyes and Sabrina dreaded more than anything a betrayal of her true feelings with regard to Black Douglas.

'You think him a spoilt man?'

'In some ways. Life was very much his oyster, wasn't it?'

'His pearl, Sabrina. His big, glistening pearl, and it's just like fate to be cruel to those who have the most to give. Now I worry so much about his future.' Laura drew an anxious sigh and her fingers plucked the rings on her left hand. 'The other night he told me that he has disposed of the jewellery he would in the normal course of events give to his wife. He insists that he will never impose himself, disabled as he is, on a young and active woman. He was always obstinate, but now . . . ah, Sabrina, it's all such a waste! He seems set on seclusion here at Snapgates, no wife, no children, none of the things that might brighten his life. What do I say? How do I persuade him? He isn't a boy to be told what to do, and we parted angrily when I tried to make him see reason. "I won't be married for pity's sake!" he shouted at me.'

Sabrina's hands tightened about her coffee cup, and she was pierced by the love and pain she could not express for her patient . . . so proud and obstinate, and caged within his yearning for the girl whom he knew to be so wrong for him.

'You must have patience with him, Mrs. Saint-Sarne. In a year or two, when he has come to terms with his blindness, he may feel differently about the future. He may start a new career, and find fulfilment in that.'

'You are forever talking about careers, Sabrina!' His grandmother looked at his nurse with exasperation. 'Nothing on earth can take the place of love, and it's love I want for Douglas. Someone who will care for him, and be with him after I am gone. I can't live more than another decade, and though you are content at present to work here you will want to go elsewhere, probably to advance that all-important career of yours.'

Sabrina flinched, for she could think of nothing more bleak than leaving Douglas.

'Forgive me, child.' Laura patted her hand. 'You looked then as if I had struck you. I suppose I don't fully understand the career girl because I was always the matrimonial type. I longed to be married and I didn't lose much time about it.'

'You must have been extremely pretty,' Sabrina smiled. 'I expect you had crowds of young men flocking around you.'

'Mmmm, it was very pleasant. I was presented at Court and I wore a delightful dress of white shantung. My hair was dark then, and dressed with real rosebuds. Yes, I was a fortunate girl. My marriage was a happy one to the very end ...' Laura gazed into Sabrina's large eyes. 'Your life to date has not been rosy, has it?'

'No, there have been briars.' Sabrina spoke lightly, but the briar scar on her cheek became at once the focus for Laura's eyes.

'I admire a girl who can stick out her chin at life, and smile at the knocks.'

'Oh, I've been a joke to myself for years.'

'It isn't really important to be pretty, my child. It's courage that matters in the end . . . but as I said before, you do so little to make yourself noticed. You tug back your hair in that unbecoming style and you wear such inconspicuous clothes.'

'They suit the person I am, Mrs. Saint-Sarne. I am first and foremost a nurse. My job is to comfort people, and my patient is not concerned with the way I look. He doesn't know if I'm wearing beige or poppy.'

'Now poppy red would suit you remarkably well.'

'So said Ret . . .' Sabrina broke off and flushed, for it sounded so familiar to speak of the nephew of the house as Ret, and to admit that he had voiced a wish, albeit a mocking one, to see her dressed more stylishly.

'Do you find my great-nephew attractive?' Laura asked.

'A girl would have to be . . .' Again Sabrina broke off painfully. 'I'm a fool when it comes to discussing men. I haven't known many, and none with intimacy. I am not attractive to men, Mrs. Saint-Sarne.'

'So you turn to a career for consolation?'

'Everyone must have something, and I'm good at my work.'

'Wouldn't you prefer to be loved?'

'I try not to live in a dream world, Mrs. Saint-Sarne. I hold to the things within my grasp.'

'Youth is the time for dreaming, not making plans for spinsterhood. What is it, Sabrina? Are you afraid of love because you think you are not lovable? My dear, I like to believe there is a partner for every young woman, because life can be lonely without someone close to you, and if you take the attitude that you are un-desirable, then you will communicate this to other people. Men are quick to spot a "do not touch" label, and it can act on the male ego like poison. Men hate frigidity.'

'I daresay.' Sabrina had to smile. 'You should be pleased, Mrs. Saint-Sarne, that with two bachelors in the house I am frigid and plain.'

'You are a bit of a mystery,' Laura said thoughtfully. 'Ret has noticed you, and if you don't watch out . . .'

'Ret likes to tease, that's all. He's rather boyish in some ways.'

'And what about Douglas? A sightless man makes up his own images, and he may think of you as a golden-haired angel.'

Sabrina laughed, 'There's no fear of my allowing such an illusion to be built up in his mind. Besides . . .'

'No image could compete with the one he carrries of Nadi? Is that what you'd like to say?'

'Yes. Did he tell you . . . ?'

'What, Sabrina?'

'That Nadi is here on the island?'

Laura sat staring at Sabrina. 'Why . . . oh, is she going to stir it all up again? The longing, the pain, the distress when she runs away a second time? Oh, why couldn't she stay away from him! She must be told to stay away . . .'

'He knows she is here, Mrs. Saint-Sarne. He's a man and his life can't be cushioned or run for him. The blows and the hurts can't be warded off. He will want to see her . . . he will want it desperately, and no one must interfere.'

'Sabrina—'

'I'm sorry to speak so frankly, but as a nurse I know that stored-up, unreleased tensions can do more harm than good. Cause him more pain than Nadi ever could. Let him have his . . . toy.'

'Yes, she is only that, when all is said and done. Even the boy knows it. He's too canny, too clever by far, to believe that she cares deeply for him. But he's also very much a Saint-Sarne and we are not a cold-natured clan. We have strong passions, and at times they rule us.'

Laura sighed and tears came into her eyes. 'When the doctors told me he was blind, I wanted to die on the spot rather than have to bear it when they told him. He took it with incredible silence, Sabrina, but his face seemed to become an iron mask. A sightless, tragic, utterly still mask. I prayed that Nadi Darrel would stand by him, but she flew into hysterics . . . she begged him to let them operate! I begged Sir Darien Williams not to do so, even if Douglas asked for the operation. I wanted the boy to go on living . . . they said that he had less than a fifty-fifty chance of surviving brain surgery, and he's only thirty-six. All the Saint-Sarne heritage would die with him, for Ret cares only about himself. Nothing would survive if he became heir to Snapgates. Everything would be sold, and the money spent within a dozen years. But Douglas . . . they call him black, but that's because he's deep, not dark-souled.'

'I know what kind of man he is—' Sabrina bit her lip, choking back the words that longed to escape; words too personal and passionate to be allowed their freedom. 'A nurse learns a lot about the patients in her charge, and I know that Mr. Saint-Sarne has lots of character, and a good deal of temper. He will shout the roof down if the door of Snapgates is kept closed on the girl he cares for. Or he may—'

'Yes, Sabrina?'

'He may shut himself in his den and refuse to see her. Either reaction must be his choice. He is still the master.'

'If she comes to Snapgates need he be told?'

'He knows she'll come,' Sabrina said simply. 'It would be unforgivable not to tell him, not to let him make his choice. He loves her, and everyone knows that love can be a torture as well as a pleasure. It holds risk as well as rapture.'

There was an acute little silence while bees buzzed madly in the cups of the golden shower, spraying down the wall near the patio table where they took coffee.

'My dear—'

Sabrina rose briskly to her feet, gathering around her the cloak of her nursing discipline. 'Mr. Saint-Sarne wanted me to help him with some letters when he returned from his stroll with Brutus. I expect he is back by now, so will you excuse me?'

'Of course, child.'

As Sabrina walked away from the table she felt Laura's eyes following her, and her heart skipped a beat. Had she given herself away? Women were so quick at catching the giveaway inflection in the voice, and it had been risky of her to speak of the rapture of love in connection with Douglas.

Oh, she hadn't asked for this, to find herself hopelessly in love with a man who didn't even know what she looked like. A man whom she desired to protect, yet who could no more be protected from the pitfalls of love than she could.

Both of them were vulnerable . . . his blindness had made him so.

CHAPTER EIGHT

It was during her explorations of the island that Sabrina discovered the cedar hut thatched with palmetto leaves, and it became at once her hideaway where she read books and changed into her bathing suit. The house pool was now ready for use, but Sabrina was reluctant to use it. It had been prepared for Nadi ... everything, and everyone, seemed at Snapgates to be waiting for her, and Sabrina was glad to get away to the tumbledown hut when her patient did not require her.

There was a cane divan, which a couple of cushions made quite comfortable, and there was seclusion, surrounded as it was by forest trees. Sometimes an inquisitive monkey would peep in, or a parrot squawk on a nearby branch. Lizards clung like tiny idols to the walls, until a gnat passed by, or something winged too close to the snapping jaws.

The floor was of coral stone, so the place was cool and could be kept clean with a house brush.

Sabrina was there on the brilliantly sunny day that Nadi Darrel came to Snapgates. She didn't know of the model's arrival until Brutus came bounding down the cliff steps in search of her and she ran to see if his master was with him.

Ret was there at the foot of the steps, lounging against a large rock. 'There you are, nurse,' he drawled. 'My cousin wants you up at the house ... he wants you to meet a friend of his. A young lady!'

Sabrina stared at Ret. She had been swimming in

117

the bay, despite the danger of casual sharks, and her hair was twisted into a damp knot, with tendrils clinging to her neck and her temples. Her shirt and jeans had sand grains clinging to them, and each thud of her heart told her that like this she was expected to meet Nadi Darrel.

Ret himself looked suave in a reefer jacket with silver buttons, pale slacks, and a knotted cravat.

'I'd rather be excused,' Sabrina said. 'Tell him . . . please, tell them you couldn't find me.'

'Why should I tell them that, Sabrina?' Ret's eyes narrowed to silvery slits. 'Douglas won't be able to compare you to his beautiful Nadi. He judges from the voice in your case . . . it's rather amusing, eh? That he thinks Nadi will be jealous of his nurse!'

'Don't!' Sabrina backed away so sharply that she didn't see Brutus sprawled near her ankles. She stumbled over the dog and fell to the sands before she could save herself. She lay prone a moment, the breath knocked out of her, and then like a cloud the sun was blocked from her gaze as with shocking swiftness, and a sort of deadly intention, Ret bent over her and pinned her to the sands with a hard, deliberate kiss.

It happened so suddenly, and was over before she could fight against him.

'You witch!' He whispered it angrily. 'I don't know what your secret is, but each time I come near you I have to try and crack that shell of yours. I – I'd like to—'

She gave him no time to say what he'd like . . . she thrust her hands against his shoulders and twisted out of his grasp, to her feet. He stood up as quickly, and they faced each other warily, like a pair of combatants.

'If you ever touch me again I – I shall tell Mr. Saint-Sarne. I won't be victimized by you!'

'Afraid of liking my kisses, Sabrina? You've not been kissed very frequently, have you, and there's a wild sort of innocence in you that drives a man—' He thrust a hand across his hair, smoothing it, and there was a strange sort of blaze in his eyes. 'It's crazy – after all there's nothing to you! You're thin as a twig, and all eyes, and you don't know a thing about pleasing men.'

'I know enough not to want your kind of attentions,' she retorted. 'You think because you're good-looking and can turn on the charm, there isn't a girl who won't fall for you. You seem to think that a girl like me should fall into your arms with fainting gratitude ... I'd rather fall off those cliffs!'

'You really are a stormy thing when you're aroused, Sabrina.' He laughed as he straightened his cravat. 'I wonder ... perhaps I should have a slight accident and become your patient? Maybe if I were helpless and at your mercy ... ?'

She scorned to answer him and bent to put on the wicker sandal which had fallen from her foot when she had stumbled over Brutus. As she straightened up the little jade charm swung out of the neck of her shirt and Ret stared at it, then swept his gaze over her sea-tousled hair.

'Do you wear that when you go into the water?' he asked.

'Yes ... have you any objection?'

'No ... and neither have sharks. They'll come to a shiny object and one of these days you might find yourself in trouble.'

'I don't swim as far as the reef, and it's here on the

beach that I seem to run into danger. Come, Brutus!'
She raced to the steps and the dog bounded beside her.
She could hear Ret leaping the steps behind her, and
when she reached the bluff, out of breath and on the
defensive, she swung to face him. 'Leave me alone,
please!'

'Please?' he mocked, and his eyes were more blue
than grey as he stood facing her, the wind and the sea
and the sky all around them. 'You are scared to be yourself, Sabrina, and I warn you I am going to drag the
real Miss Demure out of that shell you hide away in.'

'You're always making threats. The other day—'

'I know what I said, but it will be more exciting to
find out for myself why you shrink away when a man
comes near you. I'd like to teach you that it's more
exciting not to shrink away.'

'You have to prove to yourself that you're irre-
sistible, Ret. It shakes you that a wallflower like me
should resist you.'

'You are more like something that blooms wild on a
seashore, Sabrina. You look fragile, as if you'd easily
break, but you really have lots of stamina and spirit.
The Nightingale type, who'd go to the wars to take care
of the wounded, or march until you're deadbeat for the
rights of the downtrodden. You're quite a gal, when a
man takes the time to study you.'

He spoke these words with a curious softness, and for
a treacherous moment Sabrina was moved. She needed
to be told that she wasn't quite a nonentity, a hand in
the dark, a girl the eyes skimmed over to rest on a more
vivid face. Why not admit it? It hurt to be always
dismissed as the girl who was colourless.

Her eyes sought Ret's, but when he took a step forward she retreated.

'Sabrina!' He almost groaned her name. 'Won't you believe a thing I say to you? What have I got to do . . .?'

'You're bored, Ret, with the sort of girls who are used to kisses and compliments. You're wondering what it would be like to make a fool of me, but I'm not going to let it happen.'

'We'll see, nurse.' He spoke softly and his eyes shimmered blue. 'I think you've got a crush on Black Douglas, but after you've seen him with Nadi you'll realize what a one-girl man he is! He fell for her before he became blind, remember. Her face, her every smile and gesture is imprinted on his mind's eye. She is superimposed upon every image he might make of you . . . a girl he has never seen!'

As Ret's words died away all that was left was the low and insistent thunder of the surf as it broke on the coral reef below. The sunlight danced a carefree ballet on the water, shifting its peacock colours, and everything was the same as five minutes ago, and everything was bleak to Sabrina.

But Ret mustn't know, and tilting her chin she gazed back at him, at his handsome face with glinting sideburns slanting down to the cleft chin, bold curving lips and brows.

'You don't even sway from a body blow, eh?' he drawled, and he was staring at her with those strange and tiny flames in his eyes. 'Sabrina, don't waste all that dammed-up emotion on a man to whom you're but a shape and a prop.'

'I think I know my place in this house,' she said, and quickly she walked away from him, and this time he didn't follow her. She ran among the gaudy-flowered flamboyants and past the frangipani hedge, making for a side door into the house. She hoped to reach her room without being seen ... but they were in the garden court!

The peachy fragrance of the frangipani would always remind Sabrina of this moment; the hanging clusters of oleander would always look lovely and contain within them a sap that could kill.

Treacherously golden was the day, the hour, the moment when Douglas with his sharp ears caught the sound of her hand upon the latch of the half-hidden door.

'Sabrina?'

She stood very still, and then she slowly revealed herself from among the vines and the flowers.

'This is my nurse,' he said. '*Voix d'or*, as I call her to myself. I've never dared to say it aloud because she can be a delicate tartar when she likes.'

Voice of gold!

Sabrina saw the slow rising of Nadi Darrel's silky eyebrows, and in that momentary silence as a pair of green eyes looked into Sabrina's the squawk of a bush bird rose and died away.

It broke the tension ... Nadi laughed, and her eyes flicked Sabrina from her coolie sandals to her sea-marked jeans, and upwards to her face devoid of make-up, and her hair in its tangled knot. The green eyes were as glinting as jewels, and so terribly amused.

'Mr. Saint-Sarne likes to have his little joke.' Sabrina had never been so coldly calm, so withdrawn within her shell, for it was true what Ret had said. Nadi was a picture with her dramatic looks, and a filmy turquoise scarf trailing the shoulder of her white, perfectly fitting suit. 'I am pleased to meet you, Miss Darrel. I have often seen photographs of you in the fashion magazines and admired you.'

'Are you interested in fashion?' Again, like emerald wings, those amused eyes skimmed over Sabrina. Never had anyone looked so sure of herself, standing there within the reach of Douglas Saint-Sarne, almost swarthy in comparison to Nadi, so tall, the spread of his shoulders her background.

It was Laura who came to Sabrina's rescue. 'My dear, you have been swimming and would like to change before we have tea. Run upstairs and put on something nice.'

'I – I shan't be long.' Sabrina hastened away, and when she reached her room she stood very still a moment, hands clasped over her face. She gave a nervous shudder as tension released its hold on her. The girl whom Douglas loved was lovely, sensuous, exciting ... if only she had the heart to make him happy. To give generously of herself and not let it matter that he couldn't see her.

With a little sigh Sabrina opened her clothes closet, and stared at the dress that hung there. Not one of hers! It was the colour of a deep-tinted rose, and it had a deeply cuffed neckline. Then as she touched its softness with wondering fingers, she saw a piece of note-paper folded into the neck of the dress. She unfolded it and read the note:

'Lucille took the measurements of one of your uniforms, and Charles drove me into town so I could buy you the dress. Please don't be annoyed. I wanted very much to give you something pretty. Laura.'

A lump came into Sabrina's throat. Never had anyone given her such a nice surprise. She felt so grateful to Laura that tears swam in her eyes.

When at last she was dressed, with her hair knotted

smoothly at the nape of her neck, she looked and felt quite soignée. The rose-colour seemed to bring a deep sparkle to her eyes, and her skin looked velvety against the soft draping of the neckline. She didn't sigh for the pretty face she did not possess, but she wondered briefly what it felt like to be as captivating as Nadi. Wherever she went, in whatever company she dined or played, she must always be the focus of all eyes. Had it pleased or annoyed Douglas Saint-Sarne that his girl-friend should be so admired and desired by other men?

Squaring her shoulders, Sabrina made her way downstairs. She arrived to find a circular tea-table set beneath the spread branches of a tulip tree, and she at once approached Laura and whispered her thanks for the dress.

'You look nice,' Laura smiled. 'I hoped that colour would suit you, and it does, to perfection.'

'I – I was so pleased, and touched.' And then as if she felt a touch Sabrina turned sharply and met Ret's eyes. His gaze was fixed upon her, like a deliberate and half-mocking caress. He didn't say anything, but his eyes were repeating silently all the things he had said to her on the cliffs.

It wouldn't have mattered, she could have ignored him, but Nadi had noticed and was looking at them, her stunning face framed by the fan of her cane chair.

Douglas sat nearby in a similar chair, and it wasn't until Sabrina dared a look at him that she saw the rather savage set to his mouth. He was suffering not the physical pain she could deal with, but a pain of a more personal nature. A deep, crushing ache to be the man he had been, fully able to meet Nadi on all levels; a dominant, successful, fearless male, with everything to offer instead of the dependence of a blind man.

Tea and salad and a selection of homemade cakes were wheeled out to the table, and Laura made gracious conversation as she poured the English tea, especially brought to her by ship whenever it called at the island.

Everyone talked, but very little was really said. There was a surface gaiety, and undercurrents to which Sabrina was attuned, seated as she was beside Ret, whose long and immaculate left leg had a tendency to brush against hers whenever he leaned to the table to select some more delicious stuffed crab, or a slice of pineapple.

Sabrina was on edge the whole time, too uncertain of herself to know how to deal with the advances of a man she didn't quite trust. Whenever his eyes brushed her neck, enchained by Black Douglas's gift from the past, she felt the oddest sensation. Ret unnerved her, for never in her life had anyone so outrageously handsome looked at her with that sort of look.

As his white teeth bit into the slice of fruit, it was as if she felt him taking a bite at her!

Towards the end of the meal she was ready to leap to her feet and run from the tensions that were palpable. Laura was too polite to Nadi, as if she were just a visitor. His grandmother was refusing to believe that Douglas would want Nadi to come here again . . . and yet again.

Then happened what was somehow inevitable, the climax to this play on the nerves. Douglas reached for his second cup of tea, and his hand seeking in the dark sent the bone china cup toppling over, its contents spilling in all directions over the lace cloth. Even as it happened, even as the hot tea spilled and splashed, Douglas swore, and Sabrina grabbed a napkin, too well trained for this sort of mishap to be at a disadvantage. Nadi drew her elegant legs out of the way of the deluge, and all might have been well if Laura hadn't tried to take the blame.

'My fault, dear boy,' she said. 'I placed the cup too near your hand, and I overfilled it.'

'For heaven's sake, Nan!' A sudden pallor tightened the skin over his facial bones. 'I'm blind as a bat and everyone knows I'm a hazard in civilized company. I should be fed like a child with warm milk from a spoon. My apologies for my clumsiness. I hope, Nadi, that none of the tea went over your dress.'

'Not a speck, darling.' She touched his cheek in the most intimate fashion, and Sabrina, mopping up wildly, nearly upset the vase of flowers as well.

'Poor Sabrina.' Ret spoke in an amused voice. 'She always comes in for the donkey work. Watch your own dress, there's a good girl. You don't want to spoil all that soft, rosy stuff.'

A flush licked high across her cheekbones, for he spoke those words as if he would like nothing better than to touch with his fingers the soft material of the dress, and the vulnerable, very feminine person it made of her.

'Leave well alone, Sabrina.' There was a lash-edge to Douglas's voice. 'Call one of the maids to see to that! I've told you before—'

'It's all done,' she said lightly. 'I'll just run this table-cloth indoors so the tea can be soaked out of it.'

'You're very efficient, Nurse Muir.' Nadi made it sound one of the seven sins against seductiveness. 'I suppose nurses are trained never to get into a flap?'

'That's the main reason I keep her here.' Douglas seemed to need to vent his self-annoyance, and Sabrina knew that he was venting it on her rather than on those he cared for. 'She's good at keeping the blind lion under control.'

'Douglas, do you often lose control?' Nadi reached for his hand as Sabrina left the table with the soggy lace cloth in her hand. She took it to the kitchen, and tried not to be hurt because Douglas had turned on her in front of Nadi. He knew she could take it, just as she had known all along that it was madly unethical to fall in love with him. She didn't want to return to the garden court, but knew that she must. Nadi was so essentially female, and so engrossed with all the facets of being a woman, that she might too readily guess why Sabrina did not return to the party.

Suddenly the day felt cloying in its warmth, a little stormy, and it took all her resolve to traverse the frangipani walk and to go in through the little garden door.

They had left the table and taken to the loungers beneath the violet bells of the jacaranda and the coral coxcombs of the immortelle trees. The blending of colours suited Nadi, and she must have known it, for her lips were pouting slightly as she looked at Douglas, directly into the sightless eyes that could no longer express their pleasure in her looks.

'I'm intrigued by voodoo,' she was saying, 'and Ret has promised to take me to see the fire dancers. After all, I want to see everything I can while I'm here.'

'How long are you staying?' His hand was controlled and the lighter met without a blunder the tip of his slim cigar, igniting it from the concealed flame. Whatever he was feeling was equally under control, and Sabrina marvelled at the strength of will that made it possible for this man to suffer so much and to look so bland as he ejected smoke from his nostrils.

'About three weeks.' Nadi reached up a slim, lightly tanned arm, divested of her white jacket, and her fingers plucked a violet flower that drooped close to her. She caressed her cheek with it, and her green gaze drifted to Ret and back to Douglas. 'When I leave your island paradise I go on to Florida, of all places, to model winter furs. I shall die, swathed in furs in the orange groves, but *Vogue* thought it would be a charming idea.'

'What women go through for the sake of glamour!' Ret drawled. 'I couldn't imagine our Nurse Muir having much patience with all that – well, Sabrina? You're sitting there very quiet, like Alice at the Mad Hatter's tea party. What do you say to sables and oranges?'

'I'm sure Miss Darrel will look gorgeous. Each one of us, after all, is made for a particular purpose, and glamour is as important to the healthy man and woman as comfort is to the sick. It's all part of life, and life has many facets.'

'How demurely philosophical!' Ret laughed at her and there was in his voice a hint to those listening that he and she were indulgent towards each other. Oh, lord, what was he playing at? The other day he had mocked her for a mouse, and threatened to write to England for information about her. Now he flirted with her, right in front of Nadi and within earshot of his cousin. He made it seem as if he liked her when all the time he was curious about her, as a person whom he suspected of having a secret, and as a girl who had never had a lover.

'I'm sure Nurse Muir knows what she is talking about,' Nadi purred. 'She looks the clever sort to me. I'd be an absolute loss in a sickroom.'

'My dear Nadi,' Ret drawled, 'I'm sure the very look of you would be a tonic to anyone laid low.'

There was instantly one of those acute little silences in which the cicadas shrilled, like Sabrina's nerves. It wasn't always possible to guard one's words, and Ret was not over-sensitive, but all the same he might try to be more considerate. Douglas gave no outward sign that he was struck by his cousin's words; his face was as firmly moulded as a mask, and blank as some bottomless tarn were those eyes that stared at the jacaranda and did not see it. The only movement he made was to lift his cigar to his mouth, using his thumb for his guide.

Nadi was watching him, her green eyes glittering as they roved his face and his shoulders. 'I do think you manage awfully well, darling. Sometimes, if one didn't know—'

'Practice,' he said. 'I had burn marks all over my fingers when I first started to smoke blind, and I shudder to think what I looked like after shaving myself. But it's the little everyday things one needs to overcome, if one is to face a lifetime of them.'

He spoke deliberately, as if to warn Nadi that he had faced up to his blindness so far and would not risk his very life for her uncertain love. Sabrina wanted to hold him, to hug him, to tell him how brave she thought him. No girl, no matter how lovely or desired, had the right to ask a man to submit himself to dangerous surgery for her sake. It was a strange and selfish love; it was almost pagan, as if Nadi would sacrifice him rather than not have him.

Sabrina's gaze dwelt on that lovely face, with its high cheekbones, pampered skin, and long full mouth. Nadi's eyes were her most striking feature, and her dark hair had tawny lights in it. She was like a graceful cat, sleekly curved, and with slim legs meshed in the finest nylon silk. She was desirable in every way, yet she had somehow the nature of a well-bred cat. She liked to be petted, and fondled, and cared for, but in return she gave only her fascinating beauty.

'You're gentler than you were, Douglas,' she murmured.

'I am more patient, perhaps. I have sheathed the claws that wanted to tear at everyone who came near me in the beginning. My world has changed its aspect. Now the moon is my sun, the night my day.'

'Darling—' There was an actual note of pain in Nadi's voice. 'Do I bring back memories that hurt you? Douglas, that cigar is going to burn your fingers!'

'Sabrina?' A quick helpless light flared in his eyes, then was shielded by his lashes.

Sabrina touched his hand with the ashtray and he dropped the hot stub into it. Calmly she returned the ashtray to the cane table set among the loungers, and she felt Laura looking at her, signalling a desperate, silent message: 'How long must this go on? This girl is torturing him!'

'What is it like to be in darkness all the time?' Nadi asked, almost as if she remained an adolescent within that seductive body, unaware of her own naïve cruelty.

Sabrina almost hoped that he would roar at Nadi as he sometimes roared at her, but instead two deep lines etched themselves with ironic clarity in his dark face. 'Flowers have a stronger perfume, food and wine a finer flavour, music a deeper meaning. A blind man becomes something of an epicure.'

'You!' She gave a throaty little laugh. 'The lion doesn't soon forget the arena in which he made mince-meat of the sheep. You can't kid me you've suddenly become tame. You're forcing yourself to be docile, Douglas. And I—'

'Yes, Nadi?' His voice had softened and become more dangerous. 'Are you wishing back the old days? They're gone, honey! They're over and finished. My world is no longer the world we knew together. Mine has narrowed to the limits of an island, and my challenge is that step by step I shall learn to know it. Don't, Nadi, insist that I remember the things I would sooner forget.'

With these words, spoken with sudden harshness, he climbed to his feet and using his cane, as if to deliberately impose on her his dependence upon it, he made his way out of the garden court, heading for the path that led away from the house, and as Sabrina watched him go she felt a clutch of anxiety. She wanted to follow him, but to do so would emphasize in front of Nadi that he walked in a darkness which held dangers unbeknown to those who had their sight.

'Brutus should be with him!' Laura appealed to Sabrina. 'Where is the dog?'

'He probably went to the beach ... Mr. Saint-Sarne will whistle him from the clifftops.'

'Are you sure?'

'Yes ... please don't worry. You know how he hates to worry you.'

'When he's alone I have nightmares ... I picture him falling down those steps, or walking off those cliffs,' Laura said anxiously.

'I can't bear it,' Nadi whispered, and a palpable shudder ran all through her shapely figure. 'He was so strong and capable, he made other men look like dummies.'

'He's still strong, Miss Darrel,' Sabrina said quietly and firmly. 'He manages wonderfully. In some ways he is probably a more astute and certain man. His senses have become highly attuned to sounds and objects . . .'

'You never knew him before that awful thing happened to him!' Nadi looked at Sabrina almost with scorn. 'You were never a part of that world . . . it was exciting, dramatic, with something always going on. He knew so many people, and he dominated all of them. What do you know about a man like that? Douglas as I knew him would have scared the starched cap off you!'

'I daresay he would have done, Miss Darrel. But as he is now he frightens you. He isn't helpless, but he makes you feel at a loss. May I say that it isn't a pair of eyes alone that makes a man?'

'Really?' Nadi arched her eyebrows. 'May I say I shouldn't have taken you for an authority on men?'

Sabrina flushed. She was no match for a sophisticate like Nadi, but her feeling for Douglas made her leap into the breach without thinking, just as she had leapt into the briars.

'Nadi,' Ret was studying his wristwatch, 'I think it's about time I drove you to the yacht. Suddenly the sky is overcast and we might be in for some rain, and on this island it falls heavy when it likes, and heavy rain on that dark road can be hazardous.'

'I want to say goodbye to Douglas—'

'Please,' Laura spoke with abrupt authority, 'leave

him alone. It hasn't been easy for him meeting you again, and if I had my way I'd forbid you to come again to Snapgates. Go with Ret and leave Douglas in peace!'

Nadi stared at his grandmother, then threw her dart at Sabrina. 'You all seem bent on protecting him and keeping him shut up in this house, but before I left England I saw Sir Darien Williams and he wants to examine Douglas again. He thinks that after the six months' rest he has had, he may be ready for surgery. You're a nurse! You must see the possibility of this? Unless you prefer him not to recover his sight?'

'Nadi, for heaven's sake!' Ret caught at her hands and pulled her to her feet. 'You promised me you wouldn't make a scene, and now I'm darned wild with you. Come on, I'm taking you to the yacht!'

Plucking her jacket from the back of the lounger, she went with him. She went without saying goodbye, leaving silence and sultriness.

CHAPTER NINE

THE rain clouds around the sun were a sullen, eye-aching gold shot with flame, and the rising wind clutched at Sabrina as she made her way down the steps to the shore. The sea was raking in over the rocks and the sand, and spume was rising high around the peaks of the reef. The palm fronds rattled and the shaggy banana leaves waved back and forth like the ears of some large animal.

'Go and bring him home,' Laura had pleaded. 'A blow is coming up and I dread to think of him alone on the beach. Talk to him, Sabrina. He listens to you because you are not personally involved. Tell him he mustn't see that girl again . . . oh, dear Lord, *see her*. How easily one says it! How hurtful the easy words! Sabrina, go quickly before the light fades!'

Already the shadows were creeping where the caves loomed, and the waves were leaping in to cover the tracks of anyone who had walked along the sandy verge.

The beach looked deserted, and Sabrina stood by the rocks, where earlier that day Ret had kissed her and said strange things to her, and she whistled for Brutus. She whistled on the wind and it was carried away; the sound of the waves had a lash edge, and the sun in its cage of red-barred clouds was dipping lower to meet the sea.

No Brutus came bounding to meet her, and she frowned uneasily. She had looked in the den before coming down to the beach, so she knew that master and dog were together. Laura had said that Black Douglas was not in his room . . . so he was still down here. He could have wandered in either direction, to the left or the right of the bay. And the angry tide had washed away the footmarks of a man who walked with a cane, with a dog at his heels.

In that moment there flickered over the sea the soundless lightning of a coming storm, and fear flickered through Sabrina. There was no knowing what an unhappy man might do . . . and then she remembered how once before she had come looking for him and had found him dressing after a swim, in the big cave with the blocked tunnel that used to lead up into the cellars of the house.

She ran to the cave, but it was empty of his presence. On the sandy floor lay the suit he had worn at teatime, and her fingers clenched the pale grey silk of his discarded shirt.

It was madness to go swimming with a storm coming on . . . but he wouldn't know! He couldn't see the sultry sky and those slim steel forks of lightning, the kind that was extra alarming because it came without sound, like an electrical charge drawn by the water.

Sabrina hastened down into the charging surf and she gazed out towards the reef in the hope of seeing him. The waves surged in about her ankles and rose to clutch at the jeans into which she had changed. She almost fell as the water pummelled her and then receded for a brief moment. 'Douglas!' Suddenly she was calling his name in the vain hope that he might catch the sound with his sharp ears. 'Douglas . . . Douglas!'

The name echoed on the wind and then was snatched away by the growing thunder of the tide. The rising waves clutched higher at her legs and seemed to pull at her. She backed out of the churning water, fell and was soaked to her hips. 'Douglas . . . Brutus!' Her voice rose almost to a scream, for now as if in flames the sun sank and was extinguished, and the beach was bathed in a curious mingling of grey and gold, and the shore was empty but for Sabrina's thin, wet figure, shivering with nerves.

What was she to do? Her anxiety was acutely personal and she wanted to leap into the rough sea and swim out to him . . . could she make it through those waves, leaping like angry dolphins and spraying the air with spume?

There flashed through her mind a brief montage of images . . . the grey stone building in which she had grown up, the hospitals where she had trained, the homes in which she had nursed . . . never had she dreamed of this island, of meeting a man who walked in darkness himself but who switched on the sun for her. Life would not be worth much if she could never see him again, and taking off her sandals and throwing them up the beach in the direction of the cave, she ran into the angry sea and struck out for the reef.

She knew about the undertow, the sharks, the threatening storm, but she knew also that she had to try and reach him. 'Don't ever risk your neck again for my sake,' he had said angrily, but she had already risked her heart.

As the lightning played like pale fire over the sea she swam beneath the breakers, but her strength was not so defiant as her spirit and she was thrown suddenly, the breath knocked out of her, back upon the beach by a scornful wave. She lay stunned, breathless, like flotsam tossed to the shore. She felt choked with despair, for she could never get out there to him, and he might swim on and on, if he were alone without Brutus to guide him back through the water to the shore.

Stumbling, tears and seawater on her face, Sabrina made for the cave and there she sat in the shadow and flare of the lightning, clutching his cane in her hands as if like a magic wand it could bring him back to her.

The beach was black now, except for the intermittent play of the lightning, and it must have been in an interval of blackness, while the waves crashed and the wind threshed the palm trees, that man and dog came out of the sea like a pair of primeval spirits.

Sabrina sat up sharply, her every nerve on the alert as she caught the bark of a dog. She jumped to her feet. 'Brutus?' She ran from the cave into the wild darkness. 'Douglas?'

Hands, wet and cold, caught at her and again she cried his name. His fingers dug into her, and then brushed the sea-soaked contours of her. 'Little fool!' His voice lashed at her. 'Who asked you to come down here looking for me? Who wanted you? You've got yourself as wet as an eel, and if you catch your death I shall have that on my plate as well!'

'I – I might guess you'd take your temper out on me,' she cried back at him, while the wind howled around them and the rising tide charged up the beach. Brutus barked excitedly, as if this were a game they were playing. A moment more and the tide was thundering around them and they were its captives, tossed almost off their feet, until with an oath Douglas half lifted her and dragged her into the cave. The water did not come this far, and in the dark he was always the master. The hollow boom directed him, and suddenly the spray was not whipping her hair into his face.

'Brutus, inside with us, there's a good lad!'

The dog barked and followed and lashed a sopping wet tail against Sabrina. A thankful, crazy relief spiralled through her and she had to laugh or cry. Douglas shook her roughly. 'Don't you dare get hysterical,' he ordered. 'I don't want to slap you, much as you deserve it.'

'I shan't — I'm not. I'm just glad you're safe and sound.'

'You're shivering and wet through! By the saints, Sabrina, you do the maddest things! D'you take me for a child? I know these waters, blind though I am. And I had the dog with me.'

'But there's a storm coming ... there's lightning. You could have been struck!'

'Would it have mattered?' He drew a harsh breath, and abruptly he dragged her against his hard wet body. 'You must have thought so, you dedicated little ass. What have you been doing to get soaked? Come on, tell me.'

'Stumbling and splashing about like an idiot,' she confessed. 'Shouting myself hoarse ... the tide came in fast tonight and I was scared. Your grandmother sent me to find you. I've never lost a patient ... I didn't lose Billy. ...'

She broke off and her head seemed to swim ... then she pulled herself out of the wet arms of Black Douglas before she allowed all the dammed-up, treacherous longing and relief to open the floodgates of her secret self.

'Your clothes have kept dry in the cave, *m'sieur*. You should dress or you'll catch cold.

'I'm tough as a spar,' he retorted. 'It's you, my foolish child, who will take cold if you don't change into something dry. Hand me my trousers, and you can wear the shirt and jacket.'

'Oh, but—'

'But is a silly contradictory word, nurse. I can't see you, so there's no need for prudery. Strip off those wet things and don't be more of a little idiot than you have been. Letting Nan panic you! What did you both think, that I was going to drown my sorrows in the ocean?'

She couldn't answer him, for he struck too near her heart and the fear she had lived through in the past hour. As lightning flickered into the cave she found his clothes and handed him the trousers. 'Are you going to put them on over those wringing wet shorts?' she asked.

'No, nurse,' he drawled amusedly.

'Oh – fine.' She turned hastily away from him, and telling herself not to be silly, after all she was a nurse, she unzipped her jeans and wasn't sorry to be rid of their clinging dampness. A few minutes later she was a pantomime figure in his silk shirt, but after she had rolled up the sleeves it didn't feel too bad and it amply covered her slim proportions. She hung the jacket about her shoulders like a cape and buttoned it, and then all of a sudden she began to laugh.

'What's the joke?' he asked from the darkness.

'Me! I look and feel like a shipwreck victim. Your things are so large on me.'

'I can imagine. Anyway, they'll keep you warm and that's the main thing. In fact, if there's any dry wood lying about in the cave we could light ourselves a bit of a fire. I'm afraid until the tide recedes we are imprisoned here.'

'Your grandmother is going to be fearfully worried,

m'sieur.'

'I know, but it just can't be helped. It's lucky for us this cave is handy . . . now give me my cane and I'll help you search for dry wood and seaweed, anything that will burn. My cigar lighter is in the pocket of my jacket and I'm bound to have an old bill or letter in my wallet which can be used to ignite the wood. A fire will make this place seem a bit more cheerful . . . just listen to the sea battering the cliffs!'

Sabrina gave a shiver at the sound, and was glad indeed that he had suggested they light a fire. It would dispel the crowding shadows and she would be able to see his face. 'Would you have bothered about a fire if you had been alone?' she asked.

'I doubt it. It was crazy of you to come down here with the tide on the turn, but in your funny way you're not bad company. Ah, I've just found a big clump of seaweed, all crackly and just right for burning. How about you?'

'There's quite a hoard of dry wood lying about, but I dread to think of what might be lurking in the nooks into which I keep putting my hands – ooh!' She jumped back hastily as a crab scuttled and snapped at her fingers.

'What's up, Sabrina?'

'A crab nearly got me with his pincers.'

'Then let's light the fire and when we need more fuel you will be able to locate it. I'll dump my load of wood just here, and sort through my wallet for something that will catch fire from the lighter.'

Sabrina added her wood to the pile, and she stood fingering the gold cylinder of his lighter while Brutus sniffed around the cave and poked his nose into its corners. He was probably hungry, but there was no way out while the sea stormed up the beach and licked at the gap-toothed rocks near the entrance. All at once thunder struck the walls of the cave, tightening her nerves as the lightning flared over the sea and burned its cross in the sky.

'I heard you catch your breath.' Douglas spoke suddenly. 'I take it the lightning is sharp and clear. Look, I've found a couple of envelopes and their contents, but I'm not quite sure of their importance and I'd like you to glance at them. Can you see by the lightning?'

She took the envelopes and as the cave was lit up once again by one of those shining crosses she saw that she held a typed letter referring to Braille literature, and another to which clung a perfume that was spicy rather than sweet. She knew in an instant that she held a letter written to him by a woman . . . Nadi? Opened, but probably unread, because he would not ask his grandmother to read it to him, and those Sabrina had dealt with had been impersonal business letters. For a wild moment Sabrina was tempted to let it burn, then she replaced it in his hand.

'That one is personal, *m'sieur*. It's perfumed.'

'A love letter, eh?' His tone of voice was sardonic. 'Well, as I can't read it, it might as well help to keep both of us warm. Use it for the fire. I'll build up the wood, boy-scout style, and you may have the task of lighting it.'

'Thank you. It's nice to know I'm of some use.'

'Most females are of some use, one way or another.' He stood at the centre of the cave, feeling the wind as it blew in gustily, carrying sea spume with it. He took several steps to the left until he was out of the draught. 'Here's the spot, Sabrina, for our humble hearth. Hand me the dryest sticks and I'll make the wooden scaffold beneath which the dry seaweed can be placed. You'll stand ready to set light to the paper and all being well we'll have ourselves a tenable fire.'

Now the anxiety was over, Sabrina felt a sense of excitement, of conspiracy almost, in being alone with him in the midst of the storm . . . like a caveman and his mate. When the driftwood began to crackle, set fire by a love letter, she knew that not for caviar and champagne, soft lights and music, would she have exchanged this strange intimacy with Black Douglas.

'How's it burning?' he asked. 'I can smell the smoke of the seaweed like something out of a witch's cauldron.'

'The flames are leaping,' she said, and now she could see his face, dark and strong, with a wedge of shadow in the chin cleft, and the black hair rough with sea-salt above his eyes that were so lambent it was unbelievable they were blind. The firelight played over his shoulders and was lost in the dark spread of hair across his chest. Clad like that, in trousers belted close about his middle, he had a masculinity so absolute that he made Sabrina dumbly aware of her own foolish appearance in the remainder of his clothes.

'We might as well sit down on the floor,' he said. 'You had better guide me, nurse. I don't want you leaping into the fire after me . . . how cold your hand feels! Is it nerves, or are you nervous of being alone like this with me?'

'I've been alone with you before tonight,' she reminded him.

'Ah, yes, but on those occasions I was laid low. Tonight the storm has got into my veins, nurse. My swim in rough waters has invigorated me. I've always responded to danger and it's in the air tonight . . . a scent of sulphur!'

'If you are trying to scare me, *m'sieur,* because I came looking for you, out of a sense of duty I might add, then you are unkind, and unfair.'

'Men are made that way, fair Sabrina.'

'Don't – please!'

'Don't panic.' His voice was abruptly sarcastic. 'It's a difficult enough feat being a blind man without adding the indignity of trying to charm a woman one can't see. The art of seduction belongs to men who have *all* their faculties. For instance, how can a sightless man say to a girl, I do like that tiny velvet mole that clings to the side of your neck?'

'How do you know ... ?' She broke off, blushing furiously, for he could have been snatching a reference out of the air, and she had taken it personally.

'Let us say that my fingertips have eyes,' he drawled.

Her blush seemed to encircle her neck, where that tiny mole clung against her skin. When he had brailled her, his fingers had touched it and he had remembered. Nothing had ever been so shattering ... it was like one of those tiny, insignificant things a man remembered about a woman to whom he had made love.

'Please sit here, *m'sieur.*' She forced herself to speak in the cool and collected voice of the trained nurse. 'You are not too close to the fire, but near enough to be warm.'

'Do take that chilly note out of your voice, nurse, or I shall freeze.' He sprawled on the sandy floor, and Brutus flopped down beside him and lay with his nose on his paws, blinking at the smoke and warmth of the driftwood fire. Outside could be heard the surge of the sea, slapping against the rocky walls of the cave. The thunder prowled and growled at their doorway, and as the lightning cleft the sky the rain began to pour down.

'Where are you sitting, nurse?' Douglas sought her with his hand and touched her bare slim leg. 'You're not in the draught of the cave entrance, are you?'

'No . . . I'm all right.'

'Relax, nurse. I can almost see engraved on your cool young lips the words "do not touch". It's part of your trauma, eh? Just as mine is forever linked with the cry, "you can't see me . . . you're blind!" I guess women can't help it if the men in their lives have to be their mirrors.'

'I'm not like that, please believe me.' Tears stung her eyes and she blinked fiercely, as if he could see them.

'You are alone with me in a primitive place and afraid I'll make of you a punishment for Nadi.' He sighed and leaned back on his elbow. 'You need be unafraid of any such thing. You are not Nadi, so relax and warm those cold hands at the fire.'

She obeyed him, turning her gaze from his face, a mask of irony at her assumption she could be a substitute for the girl he really wanted, yet whom he would always reject because in a moment of crisis, at his bedside, she had said aloud what other women would have borne in silence.

Sabrina could almost pity Nadi. What greater cruelty than for a man to hear he was blind from a lovely girl he could no longer see!

The wind drove the rain through the entrance of the cave and the fire drove its smoke and its shadows around the walls and into the alcove where the contraband tunnel had been blocked in with large rocks.

'Are you hungry?' He spoke suddenly after several minutes of just listening to the storm, the crackling of the fire, and the little whines from Brutus as he snoozed and dreamed.

'M'mmm, I rather fancy a delicious cheese and onion pie,' she said. 'And lots of hot creamy coffee.'

'Spare ribs and sweet baked potatoes would suit me. D'you mind if I smoke a cigar, Sabrina? I suppose you wouldn't care to try one? It would take your mind off cheese and onion pie.'

'I'm sure it would, but I think I'll forgo the pleasure. Here are your cigars and your lighter, m'sieur.'

'Merci.' In the firelight he opened the slim leather case and took from it one of the thin and potent cigars. His teeth glimmered as they clenched around it, and his lighter pressed in against the end until it burned darkly red. He drew in a deep lungful of the aromatic smoke, and then let it drift slowly from his nostrils. 'Ah, you don't know what you're missing!'

'Only a dizzy head and no inclination for my supper when we are finally released from here by the elements.'

'I'm warning you it won't be for some time . . . can you sing?'

'Only nursery songs, and I don't think they're quite suitable for you or this place.'

'Perhaps not . . . then tell me about Billy and how you came to lose him.'

There was a stunned silence . . . she hadn't dreamed that he knew!

'Who was Billy . . . a dog or a budgie?'

A shudder ran all through her . . . of course, now she remembered. She had blurted the name down on the

145

shore, spun off her guard by anxiety followed by her relief at seeing him emerge from the sea with Brutus.

'Billy was a little boy I used to take care of.' There was relief in being able to speak of it, at last, here in this place to a man who could not see her face and its stricken look ... the look it had worn the day Lester Nader had angrily called her an old maid, careless of another woman's child because she'd never find a man to give her one of her own!

'Go on,' Douglas said quietly. 'This is the moment for telling, and what better confidant than a blind man? He can't look at you, he can only listen. I'm listening, Sabrina.'

'He was three years old, and so blond and blue-eyed that everyone admired him when I took him out in the push-chair. He had a slight weakness of the heart, and his parents were so fond of him that the expense of a resident nurse was nothing to them. Billy's father was in business for himself, and a lot older than his wife. He was a stern, precise, cold sort of man, except where the boy was concerned. His wife loved him, though she was so different, romantic and pretty and nervy. It was she ... she who took the boy to the park that day. She let him play on the grass while she read a novel; she was always reading them, a romantic recompense, I think, for being married merely to gratify a man with a child. When she glanced up from her book, Billy was gone. Someone had picked him up and carried him away, and his mother had been too absorbed in her love story to hear him if he cried.'

Sabrina stared into the fire and it all rushed back, the desperate panic of Bernice Nader, the way she had insisted, to her husband and the police, that Sabrina had been in charge of the boy. She had been terrified of her husband . . .

'She offered me her jewellery.' Sabrina's voice held a sad note of humour. 'I knew what a cold, savage temper Lester Nader had . . . he'd have choked her for reading novels and letting their child be carried off. Their only son.'

'So you accepted the blame,' Douglas said quietly.

'It seemed to accept me,' she said ruefully. 'For three days young Billy was missing, and Bernice was half off her head with worry and fear. She became hysterical each time her husband entered her room. I think she'd have gone quite mad if Nader had not been able to direct his anger at me. Anyway, the police worked fast and they found Billy abandoned in a bed-sitter at Bayswater. They eventually traced the girl who had taken him, to Belfast. A young Irish *au pair* who had got into trouble and – well, you can guess the rest.'

'Yes, I can guess.' Ash broke and spilled from his cigar.

'I was called before a board of inquiry and I – I don't know what would have happened to me if Mrs. Nader had not owned up that she was really the culprit. Somehow, with Billy's safe return, her courage came back . . . I could have lost my licence to nurse. Anyway, I felt pretty shaken up myself and on impulse I answered your grandmother's advertisement and came here to work.'

'Poor young Sabrina, it must have been hell for you, taking the blame for such a thing. And I can tell exactly how it happened, having experienced myself that Jeanne d'Arc streak of martyrdom in you.'

'Perhaps I should have taken vows?' Now she had talked about that nightmare episode in her career she could smile again, and be flippant. It was her only defence against the concerned note that roughened his voice.

'No, you wouldn't make a very good nun, you aren't disciplined enough. You'd fall over those long skirts each time you rushed in where angels fear to tread.'

'Even the skirts of nuns have become shorter, *m'sieur*.'

'Have they really? Strange to think that blind men live always a little in the past because they remember only the fashions and the faces they last saw before lights out.' And before his cigar butt could burn his fingertips he leaned to the flames and dropped it into them. 'Do you know the thing I miss the most?'

'There must be many things, *m'sieur*.'

'One thing is outstanding, and that is a woman's smile. I'd give a lot just to see a woman smile. It's a lovelier, warmer thing than any sunrise, especially when it comes from the heart, touches the lips, and rests in the eyes. A woman's smile is the most sensuous experience of all for a man, believe it or not.'

'I believe you, as you are very much a man.' Then she jumped to her feet, driven to escape from her own words. 'I'll collect some more wood before the fire sinks low.'

Brutus stirred and followed her, and when she returned to the fireside with her bundle of fuel she found Douglas staring into the flames he could only feel. Her heart stirred painfully . . . he sat remembering Nadi's smile, so seductive and promising, lighting up like green jewels those eyes that were faintly almond-shaped beneath the fine silken brows. When she smiled her lips were full, and Black Douglas had known those lips with his own.

'The thunder seems to be rolling away,' she said, adding some wood to the fire, and sitting down again on the hard sandy floor. 'Golly, I wish I had an air cushion!'

'Poor child.' He said it with a dry sort of amusement. 'Only my shirt is between thee and the ground. May I make a suggestion?'

'If it isn't too sardonic.'

'It's rather kind, coming from me. Spread the jacket and sit on it, and I'll keep you warm in my arms.'

In an instant she was in a panic. If she refused his offer, he would be offended. If she accepted she would be in dangerous heaven, tasting a joy that for him was merely a kindness.

'Sabrina? Putting it to the vote?'

She smiled shakily . . . even when he spoke her name she seemed to feel a melting in her bones. If he touched her in the firelight, enfolding her in those muscular arms . . .

She spread the jacket and sat on it. 'There, I'm quite warm, *m'sieur*.'

'You're a darned little prude for a nurse!' With a touch of anger he reached for her and found her with his long arms. He pulled her against him and sank his fingers into her hair. The firm beat of his heart was against her, so alive and reassuring in this storm haven under the cliffs. She could feel his skin, the hair of his chest, the hard pressure of his muscles. She was intensely aware of his touch through the silk shirt.

'Nice girls always make it difficult for a man to be kind,' he growled. 'Being chaste they immediately assume they are being chased. Like Gaul they are divided into thorns and sweet meadows, and Lord help the man who blunders among the thorns.'

'I – I hope I don't feel thorny.' Flippancy was her only weapon; while she still held to that she could fight off the dangerous longing to give herself to him. He was hungry for affection, groping in the lonely darkness for love . . . but with passion spent he would remember who she was, and he would no longer think of her as a nice girl.

'You feel as if you lived on lemon leaves and the lotus.' His hands pressed her ribs. 'Child, you almost frighten me. Only saints and angels should have a frame like yours.'

'What a very dubious compliment, *m'sieur*.'

He chuckled softly. 'In the circumstances, nurse, it's safer for you to be mostly spirit and not too much substance. I am blind and I have fasted in the wilderness, remember.'

'I – I'm sorry you were upset this afternoon. Miss Darrel is so beautiful—'

'Beauty and Black Douglas. Everyone said we were made for one another, the two halves of a talisman of love.' His sigh raised his chest against Sabrina's cheek. 'Have a little sleep, child. Though the storm is passing, the tide will not go out until after midnight.'

'Are you quite comfortable, *m'sieur*?'

'Always on duty, aren't you, Muir? Shut those vigilant eyes and go to sleep. Dream of some handome young man . . . but don't let it be Ret. I wouldn't advise you to let go your heart to him.'

'Why not?' she murmured drowsily, warmed by his closeness, and the sweet wickedness of being in his arms like this.

'Because a saint and a satyr don't mix . . . they'd give birth to artful brats.'

She laughed softly, 'I'm no saint, *m'sieur*.' He would

never know how unsaintly were her thoughts as he cradled her, treating her like a child, unaware of her as a woman.

CHAPTER TEN

THEY emerged from the cave to the witchery of the tropic stars, growing and expanding after the turbulence of the storm. The night was alive with the chorale of insects in the dripping wet trees, and they stamped the numbness from their legs before making the climb to the house. Halfway up the steps, which were tacky with wet leaves, so that Sabrina insisted upon Douglas holding her arm, they paused to breathe the night air redolent of a heady freshness following the rain.

'Are the stars out, Sabrina?' he asked.

'So many of them, *m'sieur*, they could never be counted. The sky seems afire with them, great blazing gems from the jewel box of Venus.'

'You phrase it very romantically.' His fingers tightened warm on her arm. 'I can almost see them, sparkling against the rain-washed bosom of the sky. It would be sad to be a realist without a scrap of imagination, eh?'

'It's a better thing to be a romantic, *m'sieur.*'

'And I took you for a cool and collected nurse. You enjoyed the drama of the storm, eh?'

'Once I knew that you – we were safe in the cave. And now we had better make haste ... your grandmother will be so anxious.'

'Yes, she'll be sending out rescue parties if we don't soon put in an appearance. Well, you'll have something to tell your children, Sabrina, that you once sheltered in a smuggler's cave with a man called Black

Douglas. They'll take me for a pirate.'

'Would they be so wrong, *m'sieur?*' she asked demurely, as they continued on their way to the bluff, the wind about them with its tang of ocean and reef where the coral swarmed.

'How many children do you intend to have, Sabrina?'

'Possibly a dozen.'

'That's a large family for a small girl. Won't you find them a bit of a handful? They won't leave you much time for coddling your spouse, poor blighter.'

'There won't be a spouse, *m'sieur*. Mind the flamboyants, they're hung with raindrops!'

'No spouse, Sabrina? Won't the neighbours talk when they see you surrounded by all those little infidelities?'

She laughed. 'It will be one at a time. I – I thought after Billy that it would be hard to look after children again, but since our talk I know what I want, when I leave you.'

'Couldn't you face another adult patient after me?' His voice was quizzical as they crossed the gloom of the garden and she opened the side door that led into the house.

The hall lights were still on, and when she turned to look at him she saw the irony of his expression, the lines stamped deep beside the grey, unseeing eyes. She wanted with loving hands to smooth those lines from his face. She knew that on the day she parted from this man her inmost being would be desolate, like a burned-out star. But part they must, because he loved Nadi, and she had followed him to the island, and inevitably he would do as Nadi asked. He would submit to the knife because he was not a man who could live without love in his life.

There in the gloom and the strange intimacy of the cave Sabrina had been closer to him than she would ever be again, and she knew that so alive and virile a man was made neither for celibacy nor the fleeting passion. He was the sort of man who responded to the forces of nature like a strong tree that wanted to put down roots and spread supple branches.

The fury with which he had told Nadi not to remind him of things best forgotten was an indication of how much he still desired them.

In that moment the door of the den opened and Laura hurried to embrace her grandson. Then assured by the warm, steel-chested feel of him that he was still very much alive, she turned and swept her eyes over Sabrina's pantomime appearance.

'My dear child!' She had to laugh. 'Oh, whatever happened to you? Did you fall in the sea and did Douglas rescue you?'

'It was one of those two-way efforts, Nan,' he drawled. 'Look, sweet woman, we're both clamouring for food and coffee, and Brutus could do with some supper as well. Can something be rustled up?'

'In no time at all, dear boy.' Laura dared to stroke his disordered black hair. 'Charles is on hand ... he wanted to look for you when Sabrina was gone all that time, but once the tide was in and that awful downpour started I knew it would be too dangerous. I've had the most awful visions ... I imagined the two of you drowned and carried out to sea ... oh, my poor dears, you do look wrecks! You must have hot baths and supper trays in bed, immediately! You sheltered in the big cave, I take it?'

'And we even had ourselves a fire, so we weren't too

badly off.'

As Laura jiggled the bellpull for Charles she gazed inquisitively at Sabrina, running her eyes over the masculine shirt that covered her slim body, and the crumpled jacket that hung about her shoulders. In one hand she carried her rolled-up jeans and sweater, still damp and freckled with sand grains.

Sabrina had been alone with Douglas for several hours, in a situation fraught with danger, and in Laura's eyes lay a question which brought the colour into Sabrina's cheeks.

It was such a relief when at last she was alone in the soothing water of a steamy tub, eyes half-closed as she rested her head against the rubbered rim and dreamed on the shores of mingled pain and bliss. Those hours in the cave had made her realize how much she loved Black Douglas. There was no shame in love if it was felt in the heart, and she would never love again. She knew it with every nerve in her body, and gradually she relaxed in the piney water and felt fresh and smoothed out after being covered in sea-salt and sand grains.

Douglas would be relaxing in his own bath, and with sudden, furious shyness she covered her eyes and tried to thrust from her senses the feel of his chest muscles, the crisp hair and supple skin. Close to him she had felt charged with all the danger and potency of the utterly adult male, and so lost to herself. Without even kissing her Black Douglas had taken possession of her.

She dared not think of the days that lay ahead, for come one morning, or come a sunset wild with beauty, and he would tell her that he was returning to England to see again the neuro-surgeon, Sir Darien Williams.

There in the cave she had felt in him the lonely hunger for love ... the reaching out for a life unbounded by the dark barricades of the blind. It would be different if Nadi could accept him as he was, but he knew how she felt and that was why he had gone down to the sea, like a wild hawk gone to cover. He had needed his battle with the waves, and Sabrina knew that she would never forget that moment when he had come out of the sea, the water cascading from his body, alive and triumphant in his strength.

Perhaps if Nadi had seen him . . . no, the hawk Nadi loved must have all his powers, and Sabrina felt suddenly cold as she stepped from her bath and dried herself. She put on her shortie pyjamas and her robe, a rough woolly one, and when she entered her bedroom she was a little cheered to see the cane table set for supper. Charles returned again within five minutes, carrying a tray of food, a pot of coffee, and a nice big cup from which to drink it. It was a French custom of this household never to use the *demitasse* in preference to the large pottery cup in which coffee tasted so delectable.

Charles drew up a chair for her, polite as ever, despite the lateness of the hour and the dishevelled way in which his master and the nurse had returned from the beach.

'Thank you, Charles.' She uncovered a dish and revealed smoky slices of ham, a pair of perfectly fried eggs, and hot mashed potatoes with a golden-brown surface. 'You are a wizard!'

'I trust you will eat every mouthful, nurse.' He poured her coffee and added cream. 'And may I say that it was plucky of you to go and find Mr. Douglas.'

'It was my duty, Charles.' She smiled and took several blissful gulps of coffee. 'I hope he had a good hot soak?'

'Indeed, I saw to it myself. I left him enjoying his ham and eggs.'

'Charles, you are a treasure!' She smiled up at him and surprised on his face a look that revealed the human being behind the polite and somewhat distant mask. 'What's the matter? You look so worried.'

'I venture to say, nurse, that if anything should ever happen to the master then it will be the finish of the mistress and of Snapgates. This house has stood here for many a year, and it would be a great pity to see it pulled down.'

'Do you think it would happen, Charles?'

His inclined his head gravely. 'Mr. Ret is not like the master, and there are rumours that an American syndicate would like to purchase the island for the tourist trade. An airport would be necessary and I have heard it said that Saint-Sarne land would provide a perfect airfield and amenities for travellers. The very thought makes me shudder!'

'I shudder as well, to think of all this perfect wildness destroyed for the sake of profit. But I'm sure nothing will happen to Mr. Saint-Sarne. I – I sincerely hope not.'

'Who can tell?' Charles gazed at her with unhappy eyes, as if he, too had a premonition that Nadi Darrel had brought discontent to Snapgates; a dark promise of trouble. 'Mr. Douglas has always been a very active man. Whenever he came to the island he liked to take out his boat, and we had horses stabled here in the old days. Nurse, is there any hope that an operation might . . .?'

'I can't say, Charles. I only know that it would be a great risk for him to take . . . he's blind now, but he has his strength, and his brains. If he lost those . . .' She bit her lip painfully. 'Given time he would grow used to his blindness, but it isn't for me, or even for his grandmother, to tell him what to do with his life. He's a man and he must make the choice.'

After Charles had gone, she ate her supper without really tasting it, and when she went to bed she lay a long time in the darkness feeling heavy-hearted Black Douglas must choose, for without Nadi an empty darkness must stretch ahead for him, split at times by pain, soothed at others by music or the sound of the sea. Sabrina fell asleep with the strange conviction that he had made his decision in the cave, during the storm.

The storm had cleared the air and each day dawned with a sea like unrolled yards of water silk, patchy in places where the blue had run into the jade, the topaz into the gold. Not a sail lay on the horizon at this side of the coast; a transient peace brooded, indolent and sun-hot.

Towards noon the sun was so abundant it was almost a torment. Its caress was ruthless, and the only escape from it was in the jungly heart of the garden, where the trees interlaced into a canopy of green hung with orchids and flamy bells . . . the gorgeous hibiscus, flower of love. Or in the coffee plantation, where the shade trees locked out the sun and the aroma of the ripening coffee beans was almost intoxicating.

Lucille wrenched her ankle one morning, and after bathing and binding it for the girl, and making sure she rested until the swelling subsided, Sabrina carried Ret's lunch basket to the coffee shed in the heart of the plantation. She had been inclined to avoid him and when she entered the shed, with its revolving fan and slatted walls of bamboo, he appraised her with a faintly mocking smile, his thin shirt open to his waist for coolness.

'This is an honour, that the invaluable Nurse Muir should call on me. Have you come to share the repast of a hard-working man?'

There was a cane chair beneath the fan, a box of cigarettes beside a magazine with a dashing sports car on the cover, and Sabrina was quite sure that half his morning had been spent among the illustrated engines and chassis of the latest in fast cars. She merely wished him good morning as she placed his lunch basket on the table. He came to her side and took a look at the contents of the basket. 'Yes, there's enough for two, and I've a bottle of wine in my locker. Come on, why not share the chicken and the crab patties with me? I'm feeling a trifle lonely, and you look so cool and demure. Don't you ever feel the heat, nurse?'

'Of course, but I try not to let it worry me.'

'Mind over body, eh?' His grin was wicked as he flicked his eyes over her slim neck rising from the collar of her pale mauve dress with its chalk stripes. Her hairstyle left her throat and ears coolly bare, except for the chain she wore constantly. Her skin was tanned a pale carnation and it suited her, for it contrasted with the colour of her eyes and her sun-lightened hair. Standing beside her Ret was almost as tanned as the coffee beans and so blond it was hard to believe his close kinship to Black Douglas. His brown chest was smooth; only his forearms showed the glint of fair hair.

'What do you say, Sabrina? Will you spare me an hour and share with me the chicken and wine?'

She hesitated, for his coffee workers were deep among the trees and this shed seemed very isolated, then as his lips quirked she knew he was reading her thoughts. She knew what he was capable of saying – that she didn't mind being alone with his cousin.

'Come on,' he indicated the cane chair, 'it's far too warm a day for a game of snatch. Sit down and be sociable. Let me tell you about the dinner party which Nadi is planning to give on board the yacht – which, incidentally, she borrowed for this trip from a friend of hers.'

Nadi's name (as perhaps he guessed) acted like a magnet, pulling Sabrina down into the chair. She watched him with outward composure as he opened a cupboard and took from it a bottle with a slender neck and a wine glass that was suspiciously like some fine ones kept in a cabinet in his cousin's den.

'I can swig mine from the bottle,' he said.

'No, really, I don't want any.'

'Don't be so ungracious, Sabrina, when I offer you the hospitality of my humble roof.' Ret poured wine into the glass and handed it to her. 'The wine they say is the male, the goblet female. Quite an intriguing symbolism, eh?'

'Quite,' she said, and now she held the glass by its stem she knew it belonged to Douglas, and no doubt the wine came from his cellar. Ret would not ask for these things, he would take them and derive a certain devilish satisfaction from doing so. She took a sip of the wine. 'It seems like an excellent vintage.'

'The very best,' he drawled. 'Nadi plans her party to coincide with the islanders' annual celebration to bless the yield from the ocean and the field. The saturnalia still goes on each year, even though half the population have drifted away and there's little need to propitiate the gods who put the sparkle in the sugar and the rum.

The way things are going this island will revert to jungle within a few years! D'you realize that?'

'You'd like your cousin to sell out, wouldn't you, Ret? To the Americans who want to make of the island a tourists' playground.'

'What's wrong with that? The island has abundant sun and ocean and coral beach to offer.' Ret sat on a corner of the table and sank his teeth into a fried leg of chicken. 'The trouble with you dreamers is that you think a paradise should be kept to yourselves.'

'Yes, in preference to seeing it spoiled by clubs and casinos and cars all over the place. Not to mention its wild and lovely beaches filled with the noise of transistor radios and every inch of space covered by an oiled body, and discarded ice-cream cartons!'

'Sabrina, I believe you are a snob.'

'I'm not in the least a snob. I'm a conservationist. I love beauty for its own sake, not as a means for making money.'

'Before he became blind Douglas was an expert at the money game.'

'Not at the expense of his island. Even then he wouldn't sell out to the profiteers.'

'You do defend his every action.' Ret's eyes were mocking, and yet there was a hard set to his jaw. 'Do have a crab patty. They've quite a bite to them.'

She ignored the suggestive note in his voice. 'You don't do so badly as a member of the Saint-Sarne family. This plantation more or less runs itself, so you have plenty of leisure in which to enjoy yourself. You know if you went elsewhere you would be just another good-looking young man. Here on the Coloured Lake you are important because you are a cousin of *mon maître*.'

'You aim below the belt when you fight for *mon maître's* rights, don't you, Sabrina? I believe it would suit you never to have him any different from the man he is. He wouldn't need you if he had his sight back ... or if he died.'

'When you fight, Ret, you aim to be cruel. I don't like to see a blind man taken advantage of.'

'Are you suggesting that I take advantage of his blindness?'

'Yes.' She clicked a fingernail against the wine glass and the tiny ringing note underlined her answer. 'I believe it was your idea that Nadi come here. You wanted to stir up old memories, reopen your cousin's wounds, and Nadi is perhaps the one person who can really hurt him, and make him discontented with his life.'

'You're jealous of her, aren't you, nurse?'

'It would be a silly waste of time for someone like me to envy a girl like her. I only wish she had a heart to match her face; a little more compassion and less self-interest.'

'You had better not let him hear you speak of pity. Perhaps that is why he loved Nadi ... she's all passion.'

'I know by now what he hates and what he loves.'

'When did you find out, when the pair of you were marooned by the tide in that infamous old cave?'

'I knew you would have to mention that!'

'I've thought of little else since it happened. I'm as envious as hell that I wasn't the guy involved.'

'I can only say that I'm relieved you weren't.'

'What an unkind nurse you are to me! Is it a form of self-defence, because you could like me if only you'd let yourself?'

162

'Ret, you're incredible. You remind me of the story of Apollo, who wanted to make love to every woman he met, and most of the time he succeeded, until he met Daphne who was so determined to remain virtuous that she changed into a laurel tree rather than be ravished by the sun god.' Sabrina smiled at the way Ret's fair hair flopped into his eyes, and the sheen of perspiration on his skin that made him seem rather like a bronze satyr-god. 'I know you've notched up a lot of conquests, but I don't intend to be one of them. I've told you before, my head can't be turned by your attractive lies. I'm just not pretty enough to believe a word you say to me.'

'When you talk like that, Sabrina, you give me a most curious ache. I want to shake you, and I want to compromise you so thoroughly that you'd have nowhere to go, no one to turn to but me.' His voice roughened and he took a long swig at the wine. 'I guess you know what I mean. Being a nurse can't have left you utterly innocent.'

'Ret, I wish you wouldn't talk like that!'

'Are you shocked? Well, it's long overdue that you should be told bluntly that you're an attractive girl, and most normal men would find you very desirable. Plain ... pretty? They're just words. Your trouble, Nurse Demure, is that you've been too reserved ... or too repressed. That darned orphanage, I expect. Was it called an institute for foundlings?'

'Yes, but that was long ago and it's irrelevant—'

'On the contrary, it's very relevant. You were reared in that grim place not to express your personality but your everlasting gratitude for regular rice pudding and greens. Don't laugh! It's true and you know it better than I!' Suddenly he leaned forward and with unexpected gentleness he touched her cheek. 'You regard Nadi Darrel as the epitome of attraction, don't you?'

'She's exceedingly attractive.'

'She works at it. She knows the exact cosmetics to use, and the clothes that will enhance her figure. She is in many ways a product of this artificial age. Did you imagine her inch-long eyelashes were natural? Dear Sabrina, I've seen her without—' There he broke off and with a muttered oath he slipped from the table and walked to the door. He stood there, hands thrust into the pockets of his slacks, and there was a tension about his lean body with the thin shirt clinging to the ridge of his spine. He had said almost too much, and in the silence the fan purred loudly and the coffee plantation was alive with a hundred small humid sounds.

'That sounded worse than it should,' he said. 'When I took Nadi to the yacht the evening of the storm she was in a strung-up mood and when the rain and lightning persisted she asked me to stay the night. I didn't share her cabin, nor did she share mine, and that's the stark truth. But about two in the morning I heard a splash and I ran up on deck. Nadi was in the water, swimming! I gave her a hand back on board and that's when I saw her without a scrap of make-up and the minimum of clothing. She looked like a kid, somehow. I'd never thought of Nadi as anything but worldly and a hundred per cent capable of taking care of herself, but as she stood shivering on the deck, outlined by a rigging light, she seemed stripped of all pretence and then I knew that she was scared to marry Douglas not because his blindness made him less of a worshipper, but because she needed guidance. I felt sorry for her ... it comes as a bit of a shock to see a favourite glamour doll stripped of her poise and her mannerisms, and

164

her clever little touches with brush and cosmetic pot.'

He paused to light himself a cigarette, and to thrust the blond hair away from his eyes. 'She's far less real than you, Sabrina. You I have known to the rain-washed skin from the day we met. You have eyes that need no artistic touches . . . your lashes wouldn't come unstuck after a few kisses.'

'Did you kiss Nadi?' The question had to be asked for Douglas, not for herself.

'I felt sorry for her . . . yes, I kissed her, then I took her to her cabin and tucked her into her berth. I didn't stay with her, on my honour.'

'Did Nadi want you to stay?'

'Yes.' Smoke clouded about his head.

'It couldn't have been respect for Douglas that made you leave her alone . . . or could it?'

'It was, to put it brutally, pure lack of desire.' He swung round to face Sabrina and his eyes held that strange blue haze. 'I heard next day when I returned to Snapgates that you had spent the storm with Douglas. I hated him for that . . . for being alone with you. I've imagined you in his arms, and it's true about jealousy, it does bite like a scorpion and it leaves a certain poison behind. Sabrina, you sit there so cool and proper, so serene and big-eyed . . . dammit, I don't ask for your compassion . . . I don't need it, but feel something for me or I swear I'll make you!'

'Are you threatening me, Ret, or demanding?' She stood up and tried to ignore her nervousness. She and Ret were so alone here, and she knew he was without scruple when it came to getting his own way. 'I'm really not your type, so do be sensible. I'm a prim, starched nurse you'd like to rough up, that's all. Now if you've had enough lunch I'll return the basket to the house.'

'It's for you to be sensible, Sabrina. My cousin has created an image of you which is nowhere near the truth.' Ret emphasized the comment with a down-grinding heel on his cigarette stub. 'But I can see the truth of you . . . your eyes promise the strange heaven of the cluricaun. You are a girl who knows that men can be cruel. I should like to prove to you that they can also be kind.'

'Be kind right now, Ret, and let me return to my duties. Mr. Saint-Sarne may need me for some office work.'

'Only for that?'

She tidied his lunch basket and refused to lose her temper.

'Your control is truly admirable, nurse. I guess it must be rather flattering to be thought a bit of an angel . . . but you're really one of those elusive creatures to whom the Irish give what they have left over. You must have quite a hoard by now of leftovers. A few birthday cards from kids you've nursed. A few theatre programmes to remind you of unshared plays. Some records of romantic tunes to which you were never asked to dance. Can you dance, I wonder? Will you come to the yacht party if Nadi should invite you?'

'I don't suppose she will.' Sabrina hung on to her smile as she came towards him, to where he stood in the doorway, blue devils gleaming in his eyes.

'What makes you so certain she won't ask you? She doesn't see you in the light of a rival. You're far too deep and self-contained for Nadi to realize your insidious fascination. She doesn't know that you cast spells.'

166

'Don't talk nonsense, Ret, and let me pass.'

'If Nadi invites you to this affair, promise me you'll dance with me.'

'I – I can't dance.'

'It's easy enough, like making love to music. You just give yourself to the man and allow him to make all the moves. Come on, Sabrina, make me that promise and I'll let you return to your patient.'

'Gentle blackmail, Ret?'

'If you like to call it that. Actually I'm wooing you.' And with an enigmatical smile, and that truant strand of hair in his eyes again, he bowed her out of the shed. 'Au'voir, Sabrina. Don't run too fast in all this heat.'

'Goodbye.' She forced herself to walk the path among the coffee trees that led to the house, and as his laughter fell away behind her it seemed to hold not mockery but melancholy. Sabrina bit her lip and glanced back among the trees, then she told herself firmly not to be a little fool. Ret knew all the tricks when it came to playing on a woman's emotions, and he had probably had a bet with himself, or one of his gambling friends on the mainland, that quite soon the plain and unloved Nurse Muir would be thrown off her guard by his charm and surrender to him.

Upon reaching the house she found herself rather out of breath and realized that her feet had hurried in accordance with her thoughts. It was absurd, but when she entered the hall she paused in front of a mirror and scrutinized herself, neither seeking nor granting any favours.

The eyes of a cluricaun? Perhaps. They were certainly immense enough to belong to something woodsy and odd. And now she noticed the natural bleaching of her mousey hair by the island's sunshine, and the light tan that was not unbecoming. As for her figure ... she had the hips of a boy and the bosom of a schoolgirl!

'There you are, Sabrina!' Laura came across the hall from her sitting-room, clad in a thin tailored dress with not a silvery hair out of place, and smiling. The past week had been indolent and peaceful, as if Snapgates were cut off from the rest of the island, becalmed like a ship in very still waters.

There was a sound of music drifting from the den ... a Beethoven sonata which underlined the tranquillity of the afternoon.

'Our island climate suits you, do you know that?' Laura studied Sabrina with frank and smiling eyes. 'You looked so pale and somehow forlorn the day you arrived here. I must confess that I had grave doubts about your ability to manage Douglas, but there is far more to you than meets the eye. You have a quiet way of making yourself *felt*. I wish ...' Laura broke off with a sigh. 'I know it's foolish, and more than the gods will grant, but if only our life here could be always like this, with no disruptions from outsiders!'

Sabrina knew to whom Laura referred, and had been made aware by Ret that all too soon the prevailing calmness would be agitated again by the demanding and temperamental Nadi. Tomorrow or the next day her invitation to the yacht would arrive at Snapgates, and Douglas would not refuse her, or resist his own desire to be with her. And when Nadi found herself alone with him she would put her arms around him and ask him in a whisper to please, please have the operation, if Sir Darien said this time that the danger to his life was less than it had been.

'Douglas needs a wife ...' Laura's words seemed to marry themselves to Sabrina's thoughts. 'But not that

168

girl, that model, with her short skirts and her selfish little heart. He must be terribly blind if he loves her!'

There was a sudden, almost awful silence ... the music had stopped, and instinct made Sabrina turn and look over at the doorway of the den. Douglas stood there. He was without his cane and for a startling moment Sabrina saw him, and almost knew him, as he had been before the loss of his sight. It seemed as if any second he would stride across the hall and there would be no obstacles he could not see.

He didn't move, and his features were darkly detailed and very still. 'Sabrina,' he spoke her name almost harshly, 'I have a letter which I should like you to read to me. I believe it's from Miss Darrel. I seem to recollect the scent which she uses.'

'I'm coming, m'sieur.' As Sabrina approached him, she guessed the contents of the letter and what his reply would be. He caught her footfalls and he stood aside for her to enter the den. The blinds were lowered for coolness and everything was shadowy. The fan purred high in the ceiling, its wings revolving like those of a giant moth. Then the doors closed behind Douglas and without speaking he handed her the letter.

'Open the blinds,' he said. 'Don't strain your eyes.'

She obeyed him and the sunshine came in and lit on the lovely things this room held, and on the surface of the record he had been playing.

Had he needed the tranquillity of the sonata before the turbulence to his senses contained in the words written by Nadi?

'Darling ...' the letter began, and he gave a perceptible start as Sabrina spoke the word. Her teeth caught at her lip, and she gazed at him and saw him fighting to keep his features controlled and almost stern.

'Go on,' he said, and as he listened to her reading Nadi's letter, he toyed with the little god of jade . . . blind like himself, and wiser than he could be, for love was not a wise emotion.

CHAPTER ELEVEN

THE sea was colourful and restless, with a frolicsome surf running up the cobbles to the strip of sand; the sails of sea craft scattered along the harbour were as gay as the bunting draped over the verandas of the houses, whose white walls were so dazzling in the sunshine. There was animation everywhere, and the deep, happy sound of song and laughter.

From the deck of *Lady Fay* the scene on shore was exciting, and Sabrina tapped her foot to the rhythm of calypso music drifting across the water.

They had been invited for the whole day so they wouldn't miss a moment of the fun, and right now Douglas was with Nadi on the foredeck drinking cocktails and conversing with some of the other guests she had asked to the party.

Nadi had stated in her letter that Douglas was to bring 'his little guide' and when Sabrina had demurred he had replied obstinately that it was bad enough that his grandmother should refuse the invitation. He wasn't allowing Sabrina to offend Nadi with a further refusal. So here she was, standing on the very same spot as Nadi the day the yacht had sailed into harbour.

But anyone looking across the opal water today would see a very slight fair girl clad in a rose-coloured dress, her eyes concealed behind a pair of smoked glasses. Sabrina felt too unprotected without them. Not a soul must guess, Nadi least of all, that her feeling for Black Douglas was unprofessional. No sudden smile, or anxious look, must betray her.

It was a warm, somehow dramatic day for the islanders' celebration; the sea held not a croon but a hint of temperament as it slapped the sides of the anchored yacht. Above the tall masts and rigging, where a gay assortment of flags were flying, the hot blue sky held a drift of golden clouds.

Sabrina hoped idly that it wouldn't rain, and then she went to the seaward side of the yacht, feeling a sense of unrest. She wanted to stay on board, even as she wanted to fly off, and as a ripple of laughter came from the sun-deck her hands tightened on the rail and she tried not to feel the knife-point of envy at her heart. Nadi had looked so gorgeous in her suit of pale turquoise silk, and with eager hands she had taken Douglas away from Sabrina after she had guided him on board from the launch which had met them.

'Darling . . .' Her voice had caressed him. 'Do come and meet some delightful people . . . Sabrina, did you want a drink?'

'Not just yet, Miss Darrel.' Sabrina had spoken with formality as they walked away from her, arm in arm so that Nadi could guide him without making it obvious.

'You must call me Nadi . . .' Her voice had floated back over her silk-clad shoulder, and then had lowered as she spoke intimately to Douglas.

Sabrina watched the dancing dusky tips of the sea ripples through her dark glasses, and she noticed that seabirds had left claw marks on the deck where she stood. She had never been on board a yacht before, and she wondered what it felt like to be at sea, cut off from all problems, sailing the crests of the waves.

Yes, she would rather like that . . . perhaps when she left the island she would return home by boat; one of those modestly priced banana boats that put in at various ports and had accommodation for about a dozen passengers. Today, somehow, she couldn't help thinking about her departure. Like a cloud on the horizon it had drawn closer ... and then she tensed, there against the rail, as she caught sight of two figures in the water, about twenty yards from the yacht. One was a man, his brown arms cleaving the sea. The other was long and gliding, its fin cutting the silver ripples in lethal silence.

Sabrina's heart seemed to turn over. She snatched off her dark glasses in order to see with more clarity, and realized with a clutch of fear that the pursued swimmer was Ret!

He had not come with them on the launch, but had said something about meeting a friend for a drink at the Colony. He had sauntered off, after giving Sabrina a rather sardonic smile, and now here he was in the water, a shark at his heels!

Suddenly a catamaran with a bright sail cut between Ret and the killer fish, something caught the dazzle of the sun and Sabrina realized it was a barb from a harpoon-gun aimed directly at the shark. Ret dived for the catamaran and was hauled on board, and even as Sabrina breathed a sigh of relief, she felt a flash of temper at the reckless way he laughed up at the yacht, water streaming off his brown body and his black briefs. Then he turned away to watch the flurry of ripples left in the wake of the shark.

The catamaran brought him close to the yacht and he climbed the rope ladder which one of the crew slung down, hooking it over the side. He was laughing as he swung himself over the rail.

'You'd laugh the other side of your handsome face if

you lost a limb to one of those brutes,' Sabrina stormed. 'Haven't you Saint-Sarnes any sense of danger at all?'

'Did I scare you, sweetie?' His eyes smiled wickedly and brilliantly as he slicked the wet blond hair away from them. 'It was a bet I made, that I'd swim from the Colony's beach all the way round to the *Lady Fay*. Sure, we knew there were sharks nosing about today, owing to the amount of trash that's been dumped from all these incoming boats, but I felt like doing something with a kick to it. Don't you ever feel like that, nurse? It might do you a lot of good to dare the devil for once in your dutiful life.'

'I think I did that in coming to this darned island in the first place.' She sat her dark specs firmly on her nose. 'Do you plan to attend Miss Darrel's lunch party in your black satin briefs?'

'Cute, aren't they? Do you suppose Nadi would mind? Personally speaking I don't think she'd notice today if a Scots piper in full kilted array sat down to lunch with her. She has got her way. She has persuaded Douglas to start again where they left off, and you know what that means?'

'I think so.'

'If you loved a man, Sabrina, would you expect him to love you more than his life?'

'I – I should hope I would be more reasonable than that.'

'For you it would be the other way around, eh? You'd love a man more than your own life?'

'Ret,' she spoke his name icily, 'don't you think you ought to dry off?'

'Or dry up, eh?' He grinned, and wiped the sea drops off his limbs with his hands. 'McQueen, that friend of mine, is coming over by launch for the *soirée* and he'll bring my togs. The devil guards his own, so he'll know I've survived to take a fiver off him.'

'Do you make bets about everything?' she asked.

'It adds a bit of spice to living, though I must confess I don't always win.'

'Meaning you owe money?'

'Meaning exactly that, dear nurse. D'you know something, that dress really suits you, but I wish you'd take off those dark glasses. What are you trying to hide, anyway?'

His question jarred her nerves, still shaken after his narrow escape from the shark. One day he would carry one of his crazy episodes too far and there might be no one around to give him a hand. Audacity wouldn't assist him in a real crisis; he had neither the strength nor the courage of Black Douglas.

'The sun is so dazzling on the water,' she said. 'It brings tears to my eyes.'

'Tears?' he taunted. 'Because you've had to hand over your patient to the less merciful care of Nadi? Well, there's no mercy in love, Sabrina. It has more to do with passion than pity, as I told you once before. In your innocence you'd be just the sort to mistake one for the other.'

'I'm not that childish!' She turned with relief to the white-coated steward who had been sent by Miss Darrel to say that lunch would be served in a quarter of an hour and in the meantime would Nurse Muir care to join the rest of the party on the sun-deck for a drink. She glanced at Ret, who arched an impudent eyebrow.

'Now you want my moral support, I suppose? Clad as I am?'

'You do know most of the guests.'

'You know my cousin . . . or do you? Of course I'll come with you, Sabrina. It weakens my kneecaps that you should want me.'

They followed the steward up the iron stairs to the upper deck, over which a gay awning had been raised against the noontide sun. All at once she gave way to a nervous laugh. 'We must look terribly odd!'

'You speak for yourself.' His fingers nipped her elbow. 'You're too used to thinking of yourself as a nurse, but you're not in uniform right now, you're on board a rather dishy yacht, and it's perfectly in order for the guests to parade about as if they've just come from Ascot, or the pearl fisheries.'

She laughed again, and then gave a gasp as he took her sunglasses off her nose. 'Ret . . . !'

'You won't need those under a sun-awning, my pet. Your eyes are the nicest thing about you and I won't have you hiding them under smoked glass.' And then, with impudent charm, he led her among Nadi's guests and in almost the same breath ordered a couple of daiquiris and said hullo to half a dozen people.

'Do come and sit here, and I insist upon calling you Sabrina.' Nadi indicated a deck chair at an angle to her own and the one in which Douglas was lounging. 'We mustn't be at all formal today, and I do find your name quite fascinating.'

As Sabrina sat down the other girl's green eyes played over her, rather like jewel prisms, and it was as if she said aloud: 'A name like Sabrina should belong to someone exciting and pretty.'

'Sabrina is the nurse who takes such devoted care of Douglas.' Nadi made her introduction a general one, and Sabrina was keenly aware of being looked at and assessed by several couples in extremely smart clothes, and with accents ranging from French and Italian to American. They all appeared to be leisured and comfortably off, exactly the kind of people Nadi would enjoy, worldly and sure of themselves . . . but what of Douglas? Did he like the type of person who spent most of the time being merely decorative and amusing? These people in Sabrina's opinion seemed more the type to appeal to Ret.

And as if in answer to her thoughts he carried her drink to her hand, and Nadi gave him one of her slow looks which arched her silken eyebrows. 'It's exactly like you, Ret, to do the unconventional thing. You swam across, of course?'

'Yes, and I had an escort, much to Sabrina's distress. It was a shark, and I'm sure she had visions of seeing me gobbled up. When aroused she can be quite a little tartar, wouldn't you say, Douglas?'

'I've had my knuckles rapped, once or twice.' Douglas glanced amusedly in the direction of Ret's voice, and Sabrina couldn't resist a quick look at him. He seemed relaxed, and he looked big and striking in a light grey lounge suit, somehow more dominant than the other men present, with his every sense alert despite his look of ease.

'Have you a drink, Sabrina?' he asked suddenly.

'Yes, thank you.' On her guard against any show of feeling for him, she made her voice as cool as the ice that tinkled against the glass as she tasted her drink. The clink of ice was like radar bringing his gaze to her . . . the unendurable gaze of his blind eyes. It was so unfair, her heart cried out, that a man of his intellect and vitality should be a victim of total darkness, unable to see the sparkle of the water, the gaily painted boats plying among the schooners and yachts with piles of fruit and fish for sale, and the bright bustle of the harbour.

She tried to visualize what it must feel like to sit in darkness among a group of people who could see, and she wanted to hold fast his hand to let him know she understood, and she wanted to describe things to him . . . but today he belonged to Nadi. She looked at Nadi, but instead of telling him how gay was the waterfront, how animated the scene, the other girl was talking to him as if he could see it all, her laughter and her remarks a little too vivacious.

'I suggest we all go ashore later on,' someone said. 'We shan't be part of the carnival from here . . . what do you say, Nadi?'

'I'd love to join the merriment . . . please, will a kind friend top up my glass?'

Ret's friend McQueen arrived and he went below to a cabin to change into his suit. Sabrina flicked her eyes over Douglas's face and she saw his black brows drawn in a frown.

'You'll have to excuse me from going ashore, Nadi,' he said. 'I'd be a setback to the frolics . . .'

'But, darling, we can't leave you behind!'

'You can and you will, honey.' His voice was firm as rock. 'I shall be only a liability among the celebrants, and perfectly all right here on board the *Lady Fay*.'

'Douglas, dearest man, you talk as if you're *helpless!*'

'In a crowd I am, Nadi. The noise confuses me, and I don't much care to be jostled and harried for the sake of something I can't see to enjoy.'

'My poor pet!' With a charming contriteness Nadi went to him and twined her arms about him, holding

178

his dark head against her sea-coloured silk. 'Then I shall stay with you. We'll laze on deck and enjoy the sea breezes while all these other mad fools get trampled and dusty in that carnival crowd.'

'Nadi,' he drew himself firmly out of her embrace, 'I wouldn't dream of keeping you from the fun, and believe me if I had my sight I'd be as eager as everyone else to join in. You will go and I shall brook no argument.'

'Darling bully!' She dropped a kiss on his black hair. 'Are you really sure . . . it is my first carnival?'

'Yes, child, I am well and truly sure. And now is lunch about to be served? I'm hungry enough to take a bite out of the nearest delectable female.'

'And that would be me.' With a throaty laugh, and a skimming of green eyes over Sabrina's rather pensive face, Nadi took note that the buffet table had been prepared and the steward and a boy were bringing trays of food from the galley. It was as if Nadi sensed the pang which had torn through Sabrina a moment ago, when her arms had encircled Douglas and his head had pressed against her shapely bosom. 'I thought a buffet lunch would be nicer than a formal meal in the saloon below, where it's rather warm today. In fact, sultry . . . now if everyone will help themselves? Douglas, what would you like? There's salad, giant shrimps, cold curried fish, cold slices of pork and turkey, stuffed crab, baked yams . . .'

'A big plate of everything,' he implored hungrily.

There was laughter and a happy clink of forks as everyone collected around the buffet table, where large platters of island wood held an appetizing selection of food. The coffee urn and cups were set up on a separate table, and it was instinct, rather than a direct request from Douglas, that made Sabrina go to the coffee urn and pour him a cup, to which she added sugar but no cream, knowing he liked it that way.

'*M'sieur*,' she said quietly, 'I thought you'd like some coffee.'

'Sabrina,' his smile held a hint of strain, 'are you still on duty?'

'I can't get out of the habit. Here you are.' She placed the cup and saucer firmly in his hand. 'It's hot, so take care.'

'Sabrina, I'll see to whatever Douglas wants.' Tiny sparks of green fire gleamed in Nadi's eyes as she came to his side, followed by the steward with a laden tray. 'Go and get your own lunch or there will be nothing left.'

Dismissed, and not all that hungry, Sabrina went to the table and helped herself to some cold ham and pickles, and a passion fruit for dessert. She slipped away unnoticed and found a quiet nook on the deck below and ate her lunch seated on a furled sail. She had nothing in common with the people here; only Douglas mattered, and he was with Nadi. She thought of the way he had smiled when she had given him the coffee, with a hint of melancholy as if like herself he felt out of things. She blinked at the sea and told herself it was the sun on the water that made her eyes sting. Iridescent silk, a cloak of shifting hues, lovely and languorous . . . yet with ripples where a sea creature swam below the surface, another shark on the prowl, symbolic of the tension that threaded Nadi's laughter and Douglas' refusal to go ashore with her.

Suddenly there were footfalls and Sabrina heard a voice calling her name. It was Ret, and she didn't want him to find her. Hastily she crouched beneath the folds of the sail and heard him approach, his feet in thonged sandals padding close by like a lithe cat in search of a mouse. She hardly dared to breathe, and then like pepper some fine sand grains entered her nose and she sneezed. Ret swung round and spotted her. He took a stride, leaned down and hoisted her to her feet. His face was half angry and he gave her a shake.

'You must have heard me calling you ... or were you playing hide and kiss, because if you were—'

'Ret!' Her repressed emotions on behalf of Douglas flared in her eyes, a mingling of pain and fury, and a desire to be alone with *him*, with no intruders, his nurse or his slave. 'Why don't you leave me alone? Can't you see I want to be left in peace?'

'You're hiding here so you'll be left alone with my sacred cousin when the rest of us go ashore! You plain little fool! He'll have that operation, and if it doesn't kill him and he sees again, he won't have eyes for you. You know, you must thrive on torment if you can stand by and watch Nadi touching him and cooing over him with not a tremor of the lip to betray you.'

With each word Ret seemed to grip her with crueller hands and to propel her closer to the yacht's rail. Something ominous had crept into the atmosphere; a shadow seemed to hang over the sun and the ocean had darkened to jade. Sabrina gazed up wildly at Ret and the blaze in his eyes frightened her.

'Ret, what are you doing?' She could feel suddenly the heat of the rail through the soft material of her dress, like a brand against her skin.

'For once in your life, nurse, you are going to admit to what you feel in that guarded heart of yours.' He pressed her painfully close to the rail and below them the sea still held that ominous tinge of green. 'You don't care for sharks, do you, Sabrina? They swim so silently and swiftly upon their prey, and they're down there in the sea.'

'Ret,' her voice was pitched to a note of pleading and disbelief, 'don't play silly games . . .'

'I like games of chance, Sabrina, but I don't like the trick played on me, that I should get trapped like a silly pup in those absurdly large eyes of yours! I could break you on this rail . . . come on, say it! Say you love Black Douglas! Admit it to me and I'll let you go!'

'No . . . no, Ret, you're hurting me!'

'I mean to hurt you.' His eyes held hers, mocking and furious. 'I mean to make you cry out that you can't live without Douglas, then I'll be satisfied that we're both in the same boat, punished alike for loving someone we can't have . . .'

'Let the girl go!' The words lashed the air like a whip, and they came with unexpected vibration from the stairs of the sun-deck. Ret turned a startled head, and over his shoulder Sabrina saw Douglas outlined tall and dark against the clouded sun. Her heart seemed to stop beating . . . he stood on the very edge of the stairs . . . one step more and he'd crash down them!

'Douglas,' she cried out, 'don't move – don't–'

But it was too late . . . in that precious instant when he might have taken heed of her warning and moved back out of danger, Nadi appeared behind him and caught at his sleeve. He could not have known who it was who held him, he jerked free of her and the next instant he lost his balance in his blindness and crashed headlong down the stairs to the deck where only a few minutes ago Sabrina had sat on the sail and watched the ripples where a shark glided.

Then someone screamed . . . and bright spots of

blood spattered the sun-bleached sail. Everything seemed to whirl around Sabrina, then she was free of Ret and running as through a nightmare to where Douglas lay so still.

'He mustn't be touched . . . he mustn't be moved,' she cried out. 'A doctor must be brought to him at once!'

In the hours, and then in the days that followed, there was much to do, and yet it seemed to Sabrina as if she sat an idol at the foot of her dark, hurt god and prayed away the time.

They fired the hurricane gun at six in the morning, and by noon the news was so alarming that every strong and sun-faded shutter was closed and sealed to shut out the force of the wind when it struck the hospital.

Sir Darien Williams came by jet plane to the mainland and from there he flew by helicopter to the island. Apart from his alligator case of fine, precise instruments, he brought with him a special nurse and an expert anaesthetist from London. He was a slim, sandy-fair man with keen blue eyes and strong, square-tipped hands. The nurse was a Scot, middle-aged and absolutely first class. The anaesthetist was a rather dour man with heavy, greying brows.

Hope entered the small hospital with them; a white, coral-stone building erected by a Saint-Sarne and now to witness a life and death struggle to save yet another dark Saint-Sarne . . . men strangely destined to be hurt by life and the women loved by them.

As the operating theatre was prepared, everything beyond the hospital seemed to be held in a strange, waiting calm. Out of it would arise havoc, or nothing at all. The long leaves of the palm trees hung like dry tongues in the heat, and there lay in Laura Saint-Sarne's eyes a voiceless fear.

A room across the corridor from where Douglas lay had been put at her disposal, and she had begged Sabrina to stay with her. 'I need you, child. I want you here with me while they operate, not downstairs in the waiting-room with Ret and that Darrel girl. Stay by me, Sabrina, and keep me sane with your calmness.'

No one would ever know, not even Sabrina herself, how she managed to appear composed when every beat of her heart was saying *his* name, and every atom of her, body and soul, was there with him in spirit. Unlike Laura, his next of kin, she had not been permitted to see him before they took him to the theatre.

'He lay so still, and it's always so strange to see Douglas inactive.' Laura slowly ripped a fine lawn handkerchief to ribbons. 'They have shaved off all his fine black hair . . . I wonder when it grows again if it will still be so black?'

His grandmother stared at the door, as in the stillness there came the sound of rubbered wheels fading away down the corridor, taking him to the long sterile table beneath the powerful lights, where even as the operation began the storm winds might strike the island. But Sir Darien had said that morning that they could delay no longer, not if they hoped to save him.

Was it hours later, or only minutes, when the door opened to admit a young nurse carrying cups of coffee? She whispered that the weather news from the mainland was still tense but hopeful.

'I pray God that if it comes, it will be later, when the operation is safely over. How long,' Laura appealed, 'how long altogether will it take?'

'These things cannot be hurried.' The nurse smiled gently and withdrew. Sabrina sipped her coffee and she neither tasted it nor did she notice how hot it was.

'Do you love him, Sabrina?'

The question seemed to fly with slow wings to Sabrina's mind, and when it arrived it was uncertain. She could have said no and denied all that she felt for him, and would continue to feel, whether he lived to marry Nadi, or whether he died. She gave a slow, cold shiver as an insect with long wings brushed her arm, a luminously green mantis, settling there in a praying attitude. She blew it gently from her arm and it went and settled on the teakwood shutters, as fluttering and prayerful as her heart.

'I – I couldn't help but love him,' she said, and it was such a deep relief to put into words at last (the words which Ret had tried to force from her with his torture). 'He's the first real man I've ever known, the first who ever bothered to notice me, and that's because ... because he couldn't see me.'

'Child, you mustn't think of yourself as so undesirable!'

Sabrina thought of Ret's pagan desire, which she would not call love, and the way he couldn't meet her eyes since that awful moment when Douglas had fallen blindly down those iron stairs.

'You will stay, Sabrina, when Douglas recovers ... pray God he recovers?'

'I – don't know.'

'He will need the care of a nurse ... a lot of loving kindness after all this.'

'Yes, but what of Nadi? She won't like it if I stay.'

'Snapgates is not yet her home.' For a startling moment Laura Saint-Sarne looked remarkably like her great-nephew, wilful and passionately desirous of her own way. 'You are welcome there, Sabrina, for as long as you wish to stay.'

'Thank you,' Sabrina said, but only to mollify the elderly and very anxious woman of whom she was fond. But Sabrina knew in her heart that her days on the island were numbered. If God willed it Douglas would live, and he would see again, and he would have no real need any more of Nurse Muir. She would not mope about Snapgates like Brutus, and pine for a place at the master's knee. She would leave quietly, as she had come, to carry on elsewhere with her work.

It was about three o'cock when Ret came to see Laura and to sit with her while Sabrina stretched her legs in the corridor. She walked quietly up and down, and the corridor was dim because the louvred shutters were closed. Everything was so still, and then abruptly a door swung open and a figure in a white gown emerged, tugging from his head a green-blue theatre cap. For a terrible moment Sabrina thought she would faint . . . she was face to face with Sir Darien Williams and his face was drawn and tired.

He stopped in his stride and he stared at her. 'Ah, you are the young woman I met with Mrs. Saint-Sarne. Nurse Muir?'

'Yes, sir.' Her eyes were huge, imploring, as they dwelt on him. It wasn't ethical to ask, for she was not a member of the family, and she could not have spoken the words had she tried. But her eyes had a will and a pleading of their own.

'The patient is in the recovery room, nurse.' Suddenly, almost unbelievably, the neuro-surgeon was half-smiling at her. 'He's going to get well, of course. I've never had a patient with so much will to live ... tell me, are you Sabrina?'

'Yes, sir ... oh, I'm so glad ... so glad!'

'I'm sure you are ... Sabrina.' Was there actually a twinkle in those tired blue eyes, strained after so many hours of skilful surgery? 'I could hear him muttering your name in his sleep ... and now if you will excuse me I will go and tell his grandmother that the worst is over.'

'Sir Darien—?'

'Yes, nurse?'

'Will he recover – completely?'

'If you mean will he see again – yes, by gradual stages. In about five or six months he should be a strong and active man again.'

The surgeon proceeded on his way to Laura's room, while Sabrina leaned weakly against the tiled wall. It was all over and Douglas had been freed from that awful pall of darkness. Douglas ... sleeping now and recovering slowly his precious strength ... and spending some of it *on her name*.

Hers? She slowly lifted her hands and clasped them over her face, and she swayed where she stood, and then was suddenly running away. She reached the stairs, just as the shutters shook as if a terribly strong hand had taken hold of them. At the same time a moaning sound swept across the grounds of the hospital, rising to a slow wail.

The hurricane!

It came angrily, out of nowhere, to uproot trees, capsize boats, and send flying the roofs of houses.

It lasted several hours, and it kept Sabrina in the one place from which she would have fled. Around midnight, when the winds finally abated, Douglas Saint-

Sarne became restless and when he spoke her name again they brought her to him. She stood there beside the dim white bed, and then she went to the chair that stood ready, and placed her hand in the hand that waited.

The dark, lean fingers closed around hers. His head and his eyes were bandaged, but not his lips. 'Sabrina . . .' His lips smiled faintly, and he held fast to her hand.

In the days that followed he never asked for Nadi or spoke her name, and one morning the *Lady Fay* was gone from her moorings.

'Real love,' Laura said to Sabrina, 'has to do with the heart, and Douglas found his way to yours in his darkness, like a hawk to its nest. Now all will be fine at Snapgates. There will be children there again, and I'm well content in my old age.'

But Sabrina remained fearful until the day Douglas saw clearly for the first time.

'I always knew,' he said, 'that your eyes would hold earth and heaven. Come, Sabrina, to me. Be loved, be always safe with me, as I have been with you. Safe in my heart, my arms, and my house.'

'Douglas,' she carefully held his bandaged head, 'look carefully at me, and be sure you aren't making a mistake. You cared for Nadi because she was lovely to look at. I – I thought you cared the day we went to the yacht.'

'Darling nurse,' his smile was quizzical, 'I thought you should have a little fun, that's all. You were always so duty-bound. Sweet Sabrina, I loved you when we were tidebound and for a few precious hours I could hold you in my arms and protect you. At first it was your voice that got to me, then gradually it was all of

188

you. Sabrina ... ah, Sabrina, I want all of you! You remind me of a certain prayer, do you know that?

'Longing I've sought thy nearness, with all my heart have I called thee. And going out to meet thee, I found thee coming toward me.'

FREE!

Harlequin Romance Catalogue

Here is a wonderful opportunity to read many of the Harlequin Romances you may have missed.

The HARLEQUIN ROMANCE CATALOGUE lists hundreds of titles which possibly are no longer available at your local bookseller. To receive your copy, just fill out the coupon below, mail it to us, and we'll rush your catalogue to you!

Following this page you'll find a sampling of a few of the Harlequin Romances listed in the catalogue. Should you wish to order any of these immediately, kindly check the titles desired and mail with coupon.

To: HARLEQUIN READER SERVICE, Dept. BP,
 M.P.O. Box 707, Niagara Falls, N.Y. 14302
 Canadian address: Stratford, Ont., Canada

☐ Please send me the free Harlequin Romance Catalogue.

☐ Please send me the titles checked.

 I enclose $_____ (No C.O.D.'s), All books are 50c each. To help defray postage and handling costs, please add 25c.

Name _____

Address _____

City/Town _____

State/Prov. _____ Zip_____

Have You Missed Any of These
Harlequin Romances?

All books are 50c.   Please use the handy order coupon.

Have You Missed Any of These
Harlequin Romances?

All books are 50c.   Please use the handy order coupon.